WHISPERING CANYON

Stuart Brock

This Large Print book is published by BBC Audiobooks Ltd, Bath, England and by Thorndike Press®, Waterville, Maine, USA.

Published in 2006 in the U.K. by arrangement with Golden West Literary Agency.

Published in 2006 in the U.S. by arrangement with Golden West Literary Agency.

U.K. Hardcover ISBN 1–4056–3545–2 (Chivers Large Print)
U.K. Softcover ISBN 1–4056–3546–0 (Camden Large Print)
U.S. Softcover ISBN 0–7862–8123–5 (British Favorites)

The text of this Large Print edition is unabridged.
Other aspects of the book may vary from the original edition.

Set in 16 pt. New Times Roman.

Printed in Great Britain on acid-free paper.

British Library Cataloguing in Publication Data available

Library of Congress Cataloging-in-Publication Data

Brock, Stuart, 1917–
Whispering Canyon / by Stuart Brock.
p. cm.
"Thorndike Press large print British favorites."—T.p. verso.
ISBN 0–7862–8123–5 (lg. print : sc : alk. paper)
1. Large type books. I. Title.
PS3539.R565W48 2005
813'.54—dc22 2005021521

CHAPTER ONE

The man in the small stagecoach sat loosely to let the constant jolting run without resistance through his lean body. The other passenger, a woman, seemed not to mind. She sat quite straight, her hands folded quietly in her lap, as though unaware of the steady succession of bumps and jerks.

Even though he had known her casually before, they had spoken but briefly during the two days from the railhead to the south. Now he leaned out the window and shouted to the driver.

'How far to Lace Curtain?'

The driver bent, showing a round, weathered face badly in need of shaving. 'Maybe five miles. We're starting up to the pass to the valley.' He grunted and spat, adding, 'I told you not to be in such an all-fired hurry.'

Joel Lockhart withdrew his head and leaned back. 'I've been warned again,' he said to the woman.

She turned her head, offering him a slow, grave smile. 'He's very insistent, isn't he? I received the same warning before we left. It must be as odd as its name, this Lace Curtain.'

She was a pretty woman, he thought. There was a touch of something Spanish about both her name, Juanita Bower, and her appearance. She was quite tall and slender, with a warm darkness about her that her reserve could not hide. Her eyes, in a finely molded face, were a deep brown, nearly black. Her hair was a definite black, thick and soft, and she wore it in a loose mass without a hat. On the few occasions when she smiled he had felt the power of her charm.

It was the third time he had been given a warning. First, on their starting out at the railhead when the man had taken his baggage:

'You're Lockhart, the new lawyer? I'm Sam Teel. It's a two-day ride to Lace Curtain and no stage coming back until I got a reason for making the trip.'

And the second morning, before leaving the rest stop, Teel had hitched the four-horse team and studied Joel skeptically. 'Hope you and the lady got a good reason for going. It ain't no sight-seeing trip.'

Joel had lived in this northwest mining country long enough to know men's liking for roughing up a newcomer. But there was more in this Teel's attitude than just the desire to make him the butt of a joke.

Even then he might have thought it the familiar hazing given a new man if it had not been for the letter which had led him here in the first place. He drew the letter from his pocket and spread it carefully on his knee. The sky was overcast and he had to bend well forward to read his sister's too elegant hand.

The letter was headed *2C Ranch, Lace Curtain, Washington Territory,* and read:

Dear brother Joel,

Your last letter told us of your work completed in all of those mining camps and of your dissatisfaction with such places as Lewiston and Walla Walla being already so settled. There is no lawyer here and perhaps no need of one, but when I spoke to Elmira Reeves about you, she said a lawyer is just the thing we will need very soon.

There is still a great deal of trouble here, even though the gold strike has played out and most people have left. So if you would like to do as you say, you could come to Lace Curtain. Tim and I will be pleased to have you close, as well as to know there will be a dependable man to help us.

Jed Hopper is running a freight train from the rail-head in early April and you can send a letter to us by that. Later in the month Sam Teel will meet the train with his stage, as I understand they are trying to bring a school-teacher in here. If you come, you can take the stage then.

Your loving sister,
Ellen Cardon

Joel folded the letter and replaced it carefully in the pocket of his broadcloth coat.

'I understand Lace Curtain is growing enough to need a schoolteacher this year,' he said.

She offered him her warm smile once again. 'I know,' she said. 'I'm the schoolteacher.'

Once more she was looking away and so he tried again to arrange his long body to fit the jolting of the stage.

To his surprise, she turned and spoke. It was the first time she had not limited herself to answering a question of his asking. 'A Mr. Clay Harkman wrote mutual friends offering me the position.'

He felt that she was studying him, waiting for some reaction on his part. But he said only. 'I hope you enjoy the work. It's something I wouldn't care for,' and knew he had sounded stiff and formal, though he had not meant to.

She was a strange woman, he thought. He had known her only slightly in the mining town east of Lewiston where he had lived last. The acquaintance had been just enough to know her name and to tantalize his curiosity. She interested him in all the ways a woman interests a man.

They were rising now, and the team had dropped to a slower, easier gait. Pines and firs were thickening on the low hills. He could feel the definite chill of a different climate creeping into the stage as the grade carried them upward, and he remembered from his sister's previous letters that late April was not the heart of spring this far north.

His restlessness grew as the stage continued to lose speed until, with a motion of apology to the woman, he opened the door and prepared to swing out. He caught a hand on the canvas superstructure above the door and pulled himself up and out, climbing agilely to the seat beside Sam Teel and kicking the door shut with his foot. He settled down, hunched against the surprising chill that met him.

'What's the trouble in Lace Curtain?' he asked bluntly.

Sam Teel leaned out and spat tobacco juice on the frozen ground. 'You're like Elmira Reeves, Lockhart. Want to know a thing and come right out with it.' He paused and added thoughtfully, 'Some say Clay Harkman's the trouble.'

'Who's he?'

'Owns the saloon.'

'What's the matter with him?'

'Depends,' Teel said cautiously, 'which side you favor. To some there's nothing wrong with him. Now me, I don't favor any side. I drive this mudwagon some, but mostly I shoe horses. I keep to my own business and every man's satisfied.'

'Or no man is satisfied,' Joel said, 'but yourself.'

'It's myself I think about,' Sam Teel pointed

out. ‘Now if I was to favor one side or t’other, what would it get me? The side I favored would bring me their shoeing, the other wouldn’t.’

‘What has a horse’s hoof to do with politics?’ Joel asked.

‘What has a man handling horses got to do with ’em?’ Teel spat again. ‘And who said anything about politics?’

‘It’s all politics,’ Joel said. ‘If it doesn’t start out to be, it ends up that way. In the end, men settle everything with politics.

‘What’s this about sides?’ he said, after a while. He remembered back to some of the towns he had seen grow and explode and then die. ‘Are the vigilantes riding?’

‘Ain’t none,’ Sam Teel said briefly. He clucked at the team to hurry them. ‘None needed—yet.’ He nodded his head up and down slowly. ‘Nothing there but feeling.’

The road had begun to level off and soon they were at the top of the pass, and the hills sloped downward away from them. At one point they were above the wall of trees and could see a wide, flat valley sprawled out below.

Sam Teel waved his hand. ‘Timber Prairie,’ he said. ‘That spot of smoke to the east is Lace Curtain hugging the mountains. Them hills to the west is farther and highen’n they look. North she’s all canyons. You been south.

‘She’s deep snow here winters,’ he went on.

'Not so much in the valley but ten, fifteen feet of it up here. Cuts us off some. Bottles things up.' He squinted at Joel and then leaned away to spit again. 'Never can tell what comes out of a long winter, Lockhart.'

'I make my living with words,' Joel said sourly, 'but I'd starve if I used them to say as little as you do.'

Teel chuckled, taking no offense. 'I might say something and when you see it you'll think different. Then you'll say, "That Teel's a fool," and take your horseshoeing somewheres else. A man has to look out for himself.'

'A philosophy that will fatten your belly but starve your soul,' Joel observed.

Sam Teel was silent.

Joel watched the scenery unfold as they dropped rapidly toward the plain below. At the foot of the hill the timber became thick poplars and cottonwoods along the banks of the river.

'We're going to get a welcoming committee, Sam Teel said. He pointed to his left and Joel looked, to see a man on horseback break from the timber and follow a straightline trail toward the smoke of Lace Curtain.

'Take him ten minutes straight across, and us about an hour by road,' Teel went on. He squinted at the distant rider. 'Sits his horse like Seth Markle,' he commented.

'Who's Seth Markle?'

'Works for Harkman,' Teel answered

briefly. 'You want to know a lot.'

'I'm not finding out much,' Joel told him.

Farther along, Teel said, 'Get inside and ride into town proper. It ain't every day Lace Curtain gets a stage.'

Joel laughed and swung down as he had come up.

Juanita Bower lifted a hand, pointing.

'Lace Curtain.'

Joel glanced out the window on her side. The wagon road followed the looping river, so that at the moment the town was on their left side and quite distinct in the still air. The smoke from the chimneys rose straight up, gray-black columns stretching into the paler gray of the overcast sky.

Lace Curtain huddled against the side of the mountains as if protecting itself from the vast flatness of the valley. The river swung away and then straightened out, so that the town lay between it and the mountain. A few scattered houses stood closest to the slopes, and beyond them a double row of business places. Smoke came only from a few chimneys and Joel remembered that a gold strike had built the town and he guessed that its going had taken most of the businesses, leaving empty buildings.

As they neared the edge of town he saw that he was right. Beside them was a log jailhouse with bars at the windows but no sign of life in it. Then a converted barn, which must belong to Sam Teel, since *Blacksmith* was painted on the side. There was a considerable space and then three more buildings and that was all. Across from the jailhouse and Teel's stood a big, imposing two-faced steer in the act of pawing, and beneath it was the legend: *Clay Harkman, Prop.* There was a lone shack directly back of the saloon, and it was even more decrepit than the others.

It was a desolate scene beneath the dull sky, empty and lifeless but for a small knot of people far up the street and a lone man standing before the jailhouse steps.

The man signaled the stage and, when it stopped, waddled forward. He was excessively fat, with the fatness in layers under his clothing and sagging from the bones of his face. A cigar was thrust between his heavy lips and he squinted so that the fat squeezed up, giving him the appearance of having no eyes.

He opened the stage door and crawled in, forcing Joel over against the woman. There was a smell about him as though neither he nor his clothing had been washed since their purchase. A large star was pinned to his cowhide vest. When he spoke his voice was a nasal whine that grated on Joel's nerves.

'I'm Abe Cobble, town marshal.'

The reception committee, Joel thought with flat humor. 'Mrs. Bower,' he said, introducing the woman. 'My name is Lockhart.' The smell of this man and his unceremonious entrance aroused quick anger in Joel. He added, 'Any objections?'

Juanita Bower was silent, staring straight ahead as if Cobble had not joined them. The man rolled his cigar between his lips.

'Depends if I got objections,' he said. 'This is a friendly town. I'm a friendly man.'

'Go on,' Joel said.

'Because you're a lawyer, don't try to run my business,' Abe Cobble said.

'Have I tried to?'

'Just a warning,' Cobble said. 'A friendly warning.'

'From a friendly man,' Joel added. The stage had gone by a general store marked *Reeves,* past an abandoned building and alongside a two-story log house that was obviously a hotel. Here it stopped and here the small crowd of townspeople waited to meet it.

'My grandfather,' Joel said, 'was a mountain man from Kentucky, and my father came west from the mountains to Nebraska. I came west from Nebraska. They wanted freedom, Cobble, and so they kept moving until they found it.'

He smiled and stepped across Cobble, opening the door and backing onto a board sidewalk. He leaned into the stage. 'I feel that way, too.' His hand shot out and he caught the fat man by his bulbous nose. For a moment Cobble was too startled to move and then he howled in anguish, swinging his arm clumsily at Joel's wrist. Joel kept strong fingers clamped on the nose and threw back his weight, pulling.

There was a minute of silence, then Cobble howled again and came from the stage like a cork from a bottle. Joel freed his grip and wiped his hand on his pants leg.

'A friendly warning,' he said. 'From a friendly man.'

CHAPTER TWO

The small crowd had been quiet, watching, but now someone whooped and laughter rolled out, swelling as Cobble felt gingerly of his reddening nose. He lifted his head, scowling.

'You—' he said to Joel, and broke off to reach for the gun strapped to his waist. Joel stepped toward him with a quick movement of his body, the angular planes of his face showing a quiet, cold anger.

Before he could reach Cobble, a woman strode from the crowd, swinging a parasol as if it were a club. The tip hit Cobble sharply across the wrist, causing him to pull his hand away from his gun.

'That's enough, Abe Cobble. You get back across the street where you belong!'

Joel turned to see a tall, rawboned woman. She raised her parasol again. 'Get back!' she repeated. 'Go cry to Harkman.'

The crowd laughed again as Cobble backed around the stagecoach, away from the threatening parasol. Sam Teel sat his position in the driver's seat, looking on but not speaking or indicating his feelings. When Cobble had broken into a shambling waddle toward the saloon, he stood up and made for the rear boot. From it he took Joel's baggage, handing it down, his powerful arms seemingly oblivious to the weight of the small trunk and the two packed bags. Joel eased them to the sidewalk and then caught Juanita Bower's luggage, as it followed.

From the crowd a man's voice said, 'So this is the new lawyer. You better sue Elmira Reeves for beating up the law.'

Joel straightened, seeking the man. He was in the forefront of the crowd, a squat, unkempt man, eyes watery in an unshaven face with a network of red veins on the cheeks.

He made a laughing sound and took a step forward. There was challenge in his movement, a bullying swagger that roiled under Joel's skin, angering him again.

The woman turned, her parasol raised again. 'And that's enough out of you, Seth Markle. Don't be any more of a fool than God made you.'

Joel said quietly, 'I can handle this, thank you,' and took a stride toward the man, who stood still until Joel was within a few feet of him and then, laughing coarsely, backed behind a small woman with the tired eyes of a seamstress, swung around the head of the stage and followed Abe Cobble's line of retreat.

Returning to the stage, Joel opened the door. 'Sorry you had to wait,' he said to Juanita Bower, and held out his hand to her. She accepted it and stepped from the stage.

When a heavy, grizzled man limped up and said, 'Your bags, ma'am,' she indicated them with a cool nod, continuing to stand with her hands folded quietly before her.

The woman with the parasol came close to her.

'I'm Elmira Reeves,' she said. 'You're the schoolteacher?'

Juanita Bower nodded, and when the man with the luggage went toward the hotel, she followed him, threading through the now-silent crowd of people.

Joel was looking for his sister, searching the handful of watching people without success. Elmira Reeves touched his arm.

'Ellen couldn't come,' she said. 'She asked me—'

'Is anything wrong?'

'Just busy,' she answered. Her lips thinned out in what he took to be a gesture of warning, and he bent to pick up his bags.

He went into the small lobby of the hotel and dropped them by the rough board counter along one wall. Sam Teel brought the trunk, shaking his head at Joel after he had set it down.

'It ain't my business,' he said, 'but if I was you—'

'I know,' Joel said, 'but I don't shoe horses for a living.'

The driver went out, shaking his head. The lobby was small and dark, with an even smaller dining room at the end opposite the desk and, just to Joel's left, a flight of stairs running upward into gloom. A battered sofa, a few chairs with rawhide bottoms, and a number of spittoons were scattered about the floor and that was all.

Elmira Reeves came in from the street, cast a sharp look at Juanita standing by the desk, and gave her attention to Joel.

'You have a riding temper, young man,' she said in her commanding voice. 'And a riding temper gets people into trouble.'

Joel noticed her clear gray eyes and determined mouth and chin, and he was of the opinion that here was a strong, guiding woman. He could sense her strength, but because it would be the strength of purpose he admired it.

'Would you have me run from that town wit?'

'Seth Markle?' Her lips set in disapproving tightness. 'Don't be fooled. He pretends to be short on brains, but he isn't.'

There was no answer and Joel made no effort to offer one. He leaned against the rough desk and rolled a cigarette. When he bent his head to the match cupped in his hands he saw that both women were watching him, carefully not watching each other.

He could feel the antagonism build up between them. It was like a wall, intangible but unmistakable.

The man who had carried Juanita Bower's bags limped his way down the stairs. 'I put your things in the first room to the left,' he said, and handed her the key.

'Thank you,' she said in her vibrant voice, and moved off.

Joel watched, her graceful figure until she had disappeared into the gloom above and then he looked toward Elmira Reeves.

'Now,' he said, 'about my sister.'

'Just some ranch work,' she said: 'You can rent a horse from Sam Teel and ride out there tomorrow.'

She was not the kind of woman who could dissemble, and her reticence was plain enough to amuse him. 'Then,' he said, 'I won't try to go today.'

'Near dark now,' the man behind the desk said. He scratched his chin. 'You got the rooms at the end of the hall.'

'Rooms?'

'Thought you might want one for a law office,' the man said.

Both Elmira Reeves and the man were studying him. 'If I stay long enough for that,' he said.

Elmira Reeves spoke briskly. 'You won't find a better country anywhere.' She studied Joel shrewdly. 'But this is no time for that.' Abruptly she waved her parasol. 'This is Jed Hopper, Mr. Lockhart. He drives the freight and runs the hotel. He—'

Jed Hopper gave her a dry grin. 'He'll learn about me, Elmira.' He bent, shouldering Joel's trunk. 'Give you a hand up, Lockhart.'

Joel picked up his bags and started toward the stairs after Hopper. Elmira Reeves called to him and he stopped. 'Come to supper,' she said, and he felt it was a command. 'I told Ellen I'd see you tonight.'

'Thank you,' he said.

'Six o'clock,' she told him, and marched quickly to the street.

He went on up the stairs, following a narrow hallway to the far end. There were three doors on each side and the farthest one on his right stood open. He went in, dropping his bags on the trunk Jed Hopper had placed at the foot of the bed. The room was small, with a window at the end and another to the east. There was a dresser and a bed and the washstand with a single chair beside it. The walls were of rough board nailed over the rounded insides of logs.

Jed Hopper pushed at the mattress with his hand. 'It ain't soft, but you get tired enough or drunk enough and it don't matter.'

Joel took off his coat and hung it over the chair. 'After Sam Teel's stage, a board would look good,' he said.

'After Elmira Reeves gets through talking you to death, anything'll look good,' Jed Hopper said. 'But she's a fine woman, just the same. She don't beat around any bushes—but you'll find out tonight.'

Joel moved to the side window and stood with his back to it. 'Warnings,' he said. 'I've had nothing but warnings since I got on Teel's stage.'

Hopper had shrewd blue eyes and now they laughed at Joel. 'You think we're giving you the razoo? You think that's what Markle was doing?' The laughter died out, flattening the sun wrinkles around his eyes. 'It ain't so.'

He limped to the door and, turning the crude latch, went on out. The door closed firmly behind him and Joel stared at the blank wooden panel. After a moment he turned to face the window, but it showed him only the rear yard of the hotel where there was nothing but a pile of trash and a horse barn set against a hill. The other window looked northward, up the wagon road.

He left the room and went into the one next to it. They were much the same, except that the side window in this room faced the street. Looking down, he noticed that the people were scattering. The stage had turned and was going slowly up the street toward Teel's blacksmith shop.

The room, he decided, would make a good office. But it irritated him that Jed Hopper was offering him a room before he was sure he wanted it. He shook his head and went out.

In his bedroom he went to his trunk and opened it, taking out clothes more suitable to the country than the black broadcloth he was wearing. At the bottom of the trunk his fingers found what they sought.

He drew a gun and gun belt from the trunk, putting them on the bed. Sitting down, he broke the gun, checking the mechanism against damage. It was as smooth, as freshly oiled, as when he had laid it away. Satisfied, he drew shells from the belt and carefully put five into the cylinder. He rested the hammer on empty and thrust the gun into his holster. It was an old gun; he had packed it from Nebraska, and he knew its feel and irregularities from a good deal of use.

The knock on the door jerked his head up in surprise.

He said, 'Come in,' and was sitting with the gun belt in his hands when the door opened.

A big man filled the doorway. He was tall and wide, the bulk of his shoulders denoting strength. He wore fawn-colored California pants; boots chased with silver thread, a fine silk shirt and cowhide vest. He carried a widebrimmed white hat in one hand.

His face was full and heavy, with silver strands in the black of his mustache and goatee. He moved easily into the room at Joel's inquiring nod, laying the white hat on the washstand and seating himself in the one chair. He placed his hands on his knees and leaned forward.

'I'm Harkman. Clay Harkman.'

'More reception committee?' Joel asked. 'Smoke?' He offered his sack of tobacco to Harkman, who refused, drawing out instead a short, thin cigar. Joel rolled a cigarette carefully.

'Call it that,' Harkman said, after lighting the cigar. He glanced around and tossed his match at the spittoon by the bed. 'Friendly, anyway.' He smiled, showing even white teeth. But there was no smile in the dark eyes that were fastened on Joel.

'I was met by a friendly man,' Joel said dryly. 'Abe Cobble.'

Harkman nodded. He spoke carefully, in a deep smooth voice. 'Cobble is a fool. There are a lot of fools in the world. This town has its share. And it will get more.'

Joel met the cold eyes squarely. 'Like a man who thinks it might be big enough for a lawyer?'

Harkman smiled again. 'I said—friendly.' He leaned over and rapped cigar ashes into the spittoon. 'Now we're two men of learning in a land of ignorance. I came here with the gold boom in the spring. A year ago—and no man to talk to since that time.'

There was an elusiveness about the well-chosen words that could not be caught. And, as he had no answer, Joel waited.

'I would appreciate your company at dinner this evening,' Harkman said formally.

'I've already accepted an invitation from Mrs. Reeves,' Joel returned, with equal formality. 'Otherwise—'

'Elmira Reeves is a fine woman,' Harkman said. 'A woman of public spirit. But there are a number of things on which we fail to agree.' He smiled again and dropped the dry ceremony of his tone. 'That's really why I came. Elmira will say a lot of things—some of them about me. I ask you to wait and judge for yourself.' Harkman picked up his hat and stood a minute, looking down at Joel and at the gun belt across his lap. 'This isn't that kind of a town,' he said.

Joel tossed the belt aside and got up, smiling his pleasant, humorless smile. 'I'll wait and judge for myself,' he said.

Harkman placed his hat carefully on his black and silver hair and bowed slightly. 'I always like a good man with me—but not a good man against me,' he said.

Joel gave no answer and Harkman stepped into the hall and closed the door. Joel watched it as he had after Jed Hopper's going but with a different feeling. Before, he had felt a rising impatience at a man who talked around what he wanted to say. Harkman had done the same, yet the man's charm had put meaning to the words.

'So,' Joel said to himself, 'that's Clay Harkman.' He went to the windows and pulled down the shades. Lying down on the bed, he felt the weary strain of the stage ride run through his body. He closed his eyes and slept.

CHAPTER THREE

Clay Harkman walked without hurry along the hall, drawing an envelope from his pocket as he went. He glanced back to make sure Joel's door was closed and then ahead toward the stairs. Seeing no one, he stooped as he passed Juanita Bower's door and slid the envelope beneath it.

He had determined the location of her room on his way up, simply by hearing her stir inside. Having inquired of Jed Hopper which was Joel's room, simple reasoning assured him he had not put the envelope in the wrong place.

He went on down the stairs now, fully satisfied. He nodded politely to Jed Hopper behind the desk and smiled when he received no answering nod. Outside a wind had risen and was blowing the last feel of winter against the town. Harkman squinted at the mountains, noticing the distance the snow had crept up their sides.

Full spring would soon be here. Before long miners would be coming over the pass, seeking a grubstake or already prepared to try their luck with the placers again. Harkman had studied all the possibilities of this migration, and he found in them that which he needed.

He had never been a man to trust to chance, and so a word had been sent to the south the past winter that he would grubstake. He needed miners, a hundred or more, he calculated; and though he doubted the richness of the streams in the mountains, still his grubstake would be an investment to buy something worth more than gold.

He found himself at the entrance to the saloon before he realized it. At this hour of the afternoon trade had almost halted. The long bar to his left stretched emptily half the length of the room. The dance floor was silent and dark. Only one of the poker tables at the rear was in use, and that by Harkman's own men rather than customers.

Not for long, he thought. When the flood came, the Spooked Steer would be noise-packed from morning to morning again. Then the gold dust would pour across the counter and into the pots on the poker tables. But again that was not the important thing. Money, to Harkman, meant buying the one thing worth all else: strength. The strength of numbers to be moved by his will.

He stopped before the huge man behind the bar. 'Leppy,' he said, 'get Markle and send him up to me.'

Leppy Gotch moved slowly, swinging his heavy, forward-thrust head when he walked. His upper body was like a massive keg, with long arms and broad hands hanging from either side. His belly pushed out but it was set solidly on the rest of him without fat. His dull, vacant eyes met Harkman's.

'Where is he?'

'If I knew, I'd get him myself.'

* * *

Darkness had blanketed the town by the time Joel left the hotel for the Reeves house. Following Jed Hopper's instructions, he went along a path between the general store and a sagging, desolate structure eloquently called the Miners' Supply. Elmira Reeves' house was the nearest to the store, separated from it by thirty feet of treeless, rock-strewn ground. Joel stumbled his way to the small veranda fronting the house, thankful for the lamplight coming through the windows.

The door opened and he found himself staring at a small, very young woman. 'I'm Nora Reeves,' she said, and took his arm to draw him inside.

She was slender, and she gave the impression of height by her straightness and the easy grace with which she carried herself. Her hair was a light blonde, almost a straw color in the lamplight, and she wore it to set off the attractive firmness of her features.

She laughed at his silence. 'Did you expect to find women here in buckskins?'

Joel thought of the flat valley and the mountains 'only—' He stopped. He could hardly tell her that one would have expected Elmira Reeves' daughter to resemble Elmira Reeves. But as they talked he saw something of her mother in her. There was the same determination, quiet and tense in Nora Reeves where it was vigorous and strong in Elmira. Her gray eyes looked out with steadiness and there was firmness and inflexible will in the set of her rather small mouth.

Elmira Reeves called them to supper in the kitchen. It was a warm, bright room, larger than the parlor, and painted to cover the roughness of the building materials.

The smell of the food made Joel glad he had accepted the invitation, but when Elmira Reeves spoke he knew it would be as he had expected. *A man has to pay for his food*, he thought humorlessly, and gave his attention to her.

'About your sister—there's been a good deal of trouble lately.'

'At the ranch?' Joel helped himself to the

potatoes.

'There and here,' she answered.

'Ellen mentioned trouble in her letter.' He had the feeling that they were sparring.

She was silent now, letting him carry it, and he said, 'I met Clay Harkman today.'

'A very handsome man,' Elmira Reeves said promptly. 'A very clever man, too. He can go a long way.'

Joel thought of the flat valley and the mountains cupping it away from the rest of the territory. 'Is there very far to go—here?'

Nora Reeves laughed. 'Not yet. But there can be. Our county seat is a long day's ride, and we hope for a county of our own some day.'

'With Lace Curtain as the county seat?' he asked.

'And Clay Harkman behind the scenes, running it.' Elmira Reeves' voice was roughened with anger. 'And Abe Cobble as sheriff—and Seth Markle in the legislature!' She leaned forward. 'You've seen Cobble and Markle. But have you seen Leppy Gotch? He tends bar—at the saloon—a halfwit. But he loves Seth Markle as if he were a mother. And Markle uses him for protection because he's big and stupid. Markle would see he had a job—as marshal, or at the capital. That's the kind of thing we'd have if Clay Harkman took over here!'

Joel busied himself with eating. 'So you

don't want a county seat here?' he asked finally.

'Yes—but not on his terms. Not when the riffraff out of the hills does as he tells them and elects an Abe Cobble for marshal. We'll have none of that!

'That is a divided town, Mr. Lockhart. As surely as the street cuts it, Lace Curtain is divided.

'Until last spring it was nothing. Jed and I had the store here—and that was all. We furnished goods to a few miners, some trappers and the cattle ranches. And then they found gold. They came like buzzards to carrion: miners, saloon men and their women, and Clay Harkman after them.'

The picture unfolded for him: Jed building the hotel and the freight line. Sam Teel coming with his blacksmithing and his stage. Stores and saloons rising and then sucking in drunken men and boiling them out onto the street when their money was gone. And finally—the end of the dust. The quick leaving for a new strike.

All but a few. Odd that a man like Harkman should stay in Lace Curtain—in a town where the boom had gone and the dust had stopped gleaming in the placer streams. Joel raised his head.

'Some men,' he said, 'have visions of the future.'

'They have. So have I.' She leaned across

the table. 'Lace Curtain is a silly name, Mr. Lockhart. But when I moved here I swore I would have no more sod shanties, no more log huts with dirt floors and oil paper for windowpanes. I made up my mind to put glass in my windows and lace curtains covering them.'

Nora Reeves injected her gentle tone. 'And the things that go with them. Mother wants a town with homes, a church, a schoolhouse.' She turned to Elmira. 'Give it time. Hasn't Jed already brought in five farmers? It can't be done overnight, Mother.'

'The farmers,' Elmira Reeves said. 'And the ranchers—Tim Cardon and Gil Abbey. They're the solid people. They nourish the land; they don't dig it up and leave it.'

Joel finished his meal and accepted a cup of coffee, hoping Elmira Reeves would remember her food while it was still hot.

He adjusted himself more comfortably to the straight chair, moving it back slightly from the table. Quickly she said, 'Go ahead and smoke. A man is always restless until he can.'

He rolled and lit his cigarette, sucking in the smoke with the pleasure a meal always gave it.

Elmira Reeves ate her food hurriedly, as if eating were a chore to be got out of the way with the least trouble. Pushing back her plate, she began to talk again.

'We have no time to wait!'

Joel raised his head in surprise. 'Nora is

always saying "give it time,"' she went on. 'While we give it time, the ranchers lose beef and Clay Harkman makes his plans.'

'Someone hustling to sell beef to the miners?' Joel asked.

'There aren't that many miners,' Elmira burst out. 'Last week Tim lost a hundred head. Gil Abbey lost fifty yesterday.'

'Where would anyone take that much beef from here?'

'Nowhere. It can't be got without coming through the valley,' she said. 'Snow still lies deep in the mountains. It's not beef or money the rustlers want. It's Tim and Gil. They've been here a while. They're strong in this country. They're men who want permanence and peace, not the quick riches of gold dust.'

He felt the quick rushing anger again. Not at what she had told him, but at the woman herself. Abe Cobble had tried to push him out and Elmira Reeves was trying to bring him in.

Nora Reeves frowned. 'Mother, you said you wouldn't.'

'I spoke my mind,' Elmira Reeves said brusquely. 'I always speak my mind, and I get in trouble from it. But that's the way I am.' She looked searchingly at Joel, sitting uneasily. 'And if you intend to stay here, Mr. Lockhart, you might as well know what's going on. You can't straddle a fence in this town!'

* * *

Joel left with a feeling of relief, walking slowly through the darkness to the hotel. It had been a tiring evening after a tiring day, and he would be glad to get into Jed Hopper's board-bottomed bed.

Perhaps Elmira Reeves was right, and it was a town divided. And maybe it was no place to straddle a fence. But, as he had pointed out to her, Sam Teel managed it.

'Not forever,' Elmira had answered him. 'Sam Teel is a man without beliefs. He's an empty man and he'll die an empty man.'

Before entering the hotel, he raised his head and saw that stars were shining behind a thin film of misty cloud. The night was turning brittle with clear cold.

The thud of a horse's hooves was suddenly loud on the crisp air. A rider came into sight, his head low against the night, his body wobbling in the saddle. He swung out of sight toward the river just short of the saloon.

A second rider drew rein alongside Joel, slowing to call, 'Where did he go?'

Joel recognized the voice and now, with the man close, the figure. 'Tim!'

'Joel!' Tim Cardon said. 'Meet you later. Which way did he go?'

'This side of the saloon,' Joel answered, and the horse leaped out again to follow the first rider.

He hesitated a moment, thinking of the

insistence in his brother-in-law's voice, then he turned and broke into a run.

He was abreast of the near corner of the saloon when a man stepped through the doors. He stopped, cupping a match to a pipe and then the picture was gone as Joel rounded the corner into heavy darkness.

The hoofbeats had faded, leaving no sound but that of his own running. The misted stars gave no light. He went past the rear of the saloon, slowing as he came into an open space.

The noise of gunfire was a bursting of sound in his eardrums. He threw himself to the ground. There were two quick shots and then a third. He had his bearings now and could see the flash of the gun.

It was ahead and to his left. Near, he judged, to one of the shacks behind the saloon. He rose to start that way. There was a scuffling sound and a man cursed. Beside Joel a figure rose as if from the ground.

'Where you going?'

'Passer-by, friend,' Joel said. 'Taking a stroll.' He held his hands away from his sides and turned to show that he wore no gun.

The man held a rifle, pointing toward Joel. 'Stay put,' he said. He had a high, sharp voice with a wavering crack in it.

The rear door of the saloon was flung open and light streamed out, illuminating the shack and showing three men by its front wall. Joel could see them clearly: Abe Cobble was huddled against the wall, his hands raised, his knees bent as if they lacked the strength to support his grossness. Tim Cardon's arms were locked in the strong grip of Jed Hopper, his slenderness not enough to break him free. He made a wrenching motion and swore.

'Let loose. I won't miss him again.'

Jed Hopper's drawl came clearly. 'Calm down.'

Four men stepped from the saloon. Leading them was a tall man, walking with the flapping looseness of a scarecrow in the wind. They came on slowly, guns drawn.

Joel took a step forward and the rifle barrel touched his back. 'Let it alone, mister.' the man said. He giggled, a high-pitched sound. 'This ain't your call.'

'That's Tim Cardon,' Joel said impatiently. 'And I'm making it my call.'

'I know.' The giggle came again. 'But keep outa my way, 'case I got to shoot a mite.'

Joel pushed angrily at the rifle barrel and stepped forward again, reaching the struggling group at the same time as those coming from the saloon.

Jed Hopper twisted his head. 'Tim's a little impatient, Lockhart. Don't you go getting that way, too.'

Tim wrenched at Hopper's grip and tore himself free. The light flashed on his gun, and Abe Cobble made a blubbering sound.

'Keno, he's tryin' to—'

The tall, lank man reached out with a surprisingly fast motion and brought a bung starter down on Tim Cardon's wrist. Tim dropped the gun and whirled with a catlike motion, slashing at the tall man's face with his fist. The bung starter rose again.

Joel pushed past Jed Hopper and hit the man in the ribs, bringing a grunt from him and causing his weapon to miss its aim.

'That's enough of that!' Jed Hopper called out. 'Tim, get back here.' He grabbed Tim Cardon by the arm, and Joel caught Tim by the waist and clamped a hand on his wrist, holding him.

'Keno,' Jed said to the tall man, 'take Cobble out of here.'

Keno looked contemptuously at Abe Cobble, still braced against the wall. 'You're marshal,' he said in a gravelly, deep voice. 'Arrest Cardon.'

'He's got the drop on me,' Cobble whined.

'It was too dark or I'd have aired your fat carcass,' Tim Cardon said, rage in his voice. He twisted like an eel in Joel's grip.

'You're outnumbered,' Joel said to him.

'Arrest him,' Keno ordered again. He turned to the four men behind him. 'Maybe you boys'll help.'

Joel tightened his grip on Tim. 'I don't think so,' he said. 'No one's hurt and if Cobble wants to do something, let him handle it himself. Or are these his deputies?'

'The new lawyer!' Keno said scathingly. 'Keep out of this play, friend.' He waved one long arm. 'Do what I told you, Cobble.'

Joel loosed his grip on Tim and bent suddenly. His fingers closed over the gun Tim had dropped and he came up, twisting to one side.

'Start it,' he offered coldly.

There was silence. Keno looked from Joel's face to the gun pointed toward his middle, and then back again. His eyes were small and dark, with glinting splinters of ice in them.

'You can't do it,' he said.

'No need to try,' Jed Hopper drawled. He raised his voice. 'One move and let 'em know you're there, Lem.' He spat on the ground and looked at Keno. 'Ever see Lem Happy shoot? Light or dark, it don't make any difference to him. He can pick that star off Cobble's chest 'thout mussing his shirt.'

From the darkness came a giggle. 'Want I should do it, Jed?'

Keno rammed the bung starter fiercely into one palm. 'All right for now,' he said in his strange voice. 'For now, Hopper.' He turned to the men. 'Get back inside.'

A man whose long trunk and very short legs gave him a deformed look swore sharply. 'They're running you off.'

'My orders, Wolf!' Keno said hoarsely. 'I said —inside.'

The man swore again and turned. Keno

waited until he saw they were doing as told and then he followed, taking Abe Cobble along.

'Cardon shows in this town again and he goes into the jailhouse,' he called back, and drew the door shut behind him.

The light blotted out, leaving the small group in silence. Jed Hopper spoke and the man with the rifle joined them.

'I think,' Jed Hopper told Joel, 'you better hang onto that gun. Tim's feisty enough to chase Cobble right inside.'

'Not now,' Tim Cardon said. 'There'll come another time.'

'You won't catch Abe Cobble alone again if he can help it,' Jed Hopper said dryly.

They walked toward the hotel, Tim leading his horse and Lem Happy trailing, his rifle in the crook of his arm. At the corner of the saloon a match flared up, stopping them. The man who had come out earlier to light his pipe was there.

'Had it covered from here,' he said.

'Thanks, Abel,' Jed Hopper said. 'Coming over?'

'Not tonight.' The match went out and the man fell in step beside them. 'Gave me a thirst, watching,' he said, and turned to the saloon as they reached the street.

'Abel Kine,' Jed said to Joel. 'A good man to have behind you.'

Tim hitch-reined his horse in front of the

hotel and followed the others inside. Back of the hotel lobby was the kitchen, and Jed led them in there, lighting a lamp and then turning to his stove to build a fire.

Tim Cardon's face was lined with weariness but he managed a familiar wide grin. 'You came at the right time,' he said to Joel.

'It looks,' Jed Hopper remarked from the stove, 'like you made a choice.

Joel had been thinking of this. 'No choice,' he said.

'You can't straddle a fence where there's only open range,' Jed Hopper said, laughing at his own joke. 'Lem, you take a mosey and see if Keno's letting it lay. And you might put up Tim's horse. He ain't riding out tonight—not alone.'

Lem Happy came back as Jed was pouring coffee. He took a seat at the kitchen table, a gaunt man who moved with the odd softness of the old-timer. He propped his rifle, an ancient Sharps, against the table beside him.

'No,' he said.

Looking at him, Joel saw the one eye was empty of life but the other was a washed blue and carried a sparkle as if the old man found everything he saw amusing.

'Lem and me been together a long time,' Jed Hopper said, noticing Joel. 'That missing eye don't mean much. What Lem don't see ain't worth seeing and what he don't hear ain't worth hearing. Lem ain't never liked anything so much as us going partners on this hotel.' He dropped his voice slightly. 'And he'll do most anything to keep it the way it is—his and mine.'

'It's good to have something to tie to,' Joel agreed.

Hopper nodded and turned to Tim Cardon. 'That was a fool thing, running Cobble down that way,' he said. 'We ain't ready to start a fight.'

Tim was blowing on his coffee. He raised his head, his mouth stubborn. 'I cut sign,' he said. 'I lost thirty more head today, and when I cut the sign I came onto Abe Cobble. What would you have me do—ask him to arrest himself?'

'Cobble,' Hopper said, with contempt. 'You think Cobble's handling this rustling? There ain't a horse alive could carry that lard enough to drive cattle off your range. And if you did shoot Cobble, what'd you have?'

'One gone,' Tim Cardon said.

'And a hundred more like him Harkman can hire.'

'You're sure its Harkman?' Joel asked.

'No,' Jed Hopper admitted. 'Elmira's sure, and sometimes I guess I let her do my thinking for me. It just smells that way to me.' He turned the full force of his shrewd blue eyes on Joel. 'Maybe it ain't Harkman, but you got yourself a side whether you want it or not. Because it's Keno, no matter how you look at it. And Keno manages Harkman's saloon.'

'I have no side,' Joel said again.

Jed Hopper laughed and Lem Happy joined in with his giggle. 'You think Keno is going to love you for smashing his ribs and then making a play with that gun, Lockhart? You come in town and spend the first evening at Elmira's. You walk out and help Tim here. Seeing Tim's your relative, it ain't going to strain Keno much to figure which side you're playing.'

Tim Cardon sipped his coffee. 'I can use some help, Joel.' He met Joel's dark gaze and grinned. 'You never were a man to be told what to do. But I'm not telling you; I'm just asking you.'

Jed Hopper took out a sack of tobacco and passed it around. 'This ain't your town, Lockhart, and it ain't your fight. But after tonight, *they'll* think you made it your fight.' He took the tobacco back after Joel had made a cigarette, and filled a pipe. 'You got to see it that way or ride out.'

'Not tonight I don't have to see it,' Joel said abruptly. He stood up. 'I'll ride out tomorrow, Tim.'

He went out of the kitchen and up the stairs to his room. Inside, he bolted the door and struck a match to find the lamp. His gun and belt still lay on the bed and he picked them up, running his fingers thoughtfully over the leather and the metal.

'Choose or ride out,' he said aloud.

He undressed and crawled into bed and

blew out the lamp. He lay motionless, staring into the darkness. Jed Hopper was right. Keno would think only one thing. Any man would.

After a while he rose and got his gun. He pushed it under his pillow before he turned over to sleep.

CHAPTER FOUR

When she heard the sound of horses' hooves coming, Juanita Bower paused in her undressing and listened a moment.

Then she let down her hair and began a slow, steady brushing, the heavy cascade of hair reaching below her waist.

The mirror before which she worked reflected her face. With her hair loose, she looked very young. She thought of herself that way until she bent forward and peered into her own eyes.

'No, not young,' she said aloud. She was twenty-nine, and much of those years was reflected in the dark, somber depths of her eyes. She remembered another person with the completeness of his life in his eyes. He was very nice, and she spent a moment thinking about him as he had been in the stage today and in the town where she had known him.

He had been nice to her, always. And she had enjoyed his obvious admiration, though until the stage ride he had never spoken more than to say hello. The thought caused her to smile, and she wondered if any woman ever grew too weary or too frightened of what lay ahead to appreciate the attentions of a man.

When the shots came, the picture of Joel left her abruptly. Brush in hand, she hurried to the window overlooking the street. She drew up the shade and looked in the direction of the sound. Two more shots followed in rapid succession.

She stood away from the window to blow out the lamp. Then, in darkness, she returned to the window, throwing it up and leaning out so that she might see toward the saloon.

Once she said, 'Clay,' very softly, and the realization of what this night's action could mean forced the tenderness from her lips.

She thought of the note he had slid under her door and the picture of other situations like this came back to her. She knew what would come next; step by step it would be the same as it had been before.

She heard voices now, and footsteps as of a number of men coming along the hard earth.

The thin clarity of the air carried the sounds to her and she caught the words, 'Abel Kine, a good man to have behind you,' but that was all. Soon they were passing beneath her window but no one spoke again, and then they were inside.

She lowered the window and the shade and

hesitated briefly by the lamp. It would be best to light it, she decided, and did so. Then she slipped quietly from the room and onto the stairs leading to the lobby.

Her dressing gown was a dark red and not easily seen in the dark. She stood without fear at the point where the stairs turned, listening openly.

She was in time to hear a strange voice mention the name of Abe Cobble, and it recalled the fat man who had invited himself into the stage. She smiled slightly, remembering Joel Lockhart's action against the marshal, but the smile died as Jed Hopper drawled out the name of Harkman. She continued to listen, each word coming clearly up from the kitchen.

They were not sure, she realized. As yet, they did not understand the full picture of what Clay meant to do. And so, for now, he was safe.

She heard Joel Lockhart deny any affiliation, either with Clay or against him, and she hurried silently back up the stairs, closing the door as he began the ascent. She leaned against the door, her heart pounding but the feel of her skin clammy with the cold sweat of fear.

In bed she lay a long while, staring at the unseen ceiling, her eyes wide open.

Always this once more, she thought. He never failed to say that this time was the time.

Even in the brief note she had received, ordering her to come quietly to him the next night, he had added that sentence: 'This time it cannot fail.'

Perhaps, she thought, if a man tried often enough, he would succeed. Or perhaps he was one of those the hand of success would never touch—if so, they would go on, endlessly repeating the pattern of the past ten years.

Her strength gave out and she turned her face into the pillow and wept silently.

Joel and Tim Cardon followed the road north from Lace Curtain. It was a crisp, cold morning with the last of winter still in the air. The sun had not yet risen over the eastern range, high at their right shoulders, but the daylight was nearly complete and fine for riding.

The road here followed the edge of the mountains, just far enough from them to be on the flats, and in a straight line instead of twisting with the river. To their left, smoke plumed upward from the farmhouses, lying naked on the bald prairie of the river valley.

'Jed brought the farmers in here,' Tim Cardon said. 'There'll be more this summer, too. It's a good land for grain and the river can be turned to irrigate if its needed.'

'You sound glad to see them,' Joel said. He rode loosely, a man accustomed to the saddle, even though it was not part of his everyday work. 'You're the first cattleman I ever saw who wanted a homesteader in his front yard.'

Tim gave Joel his familiar grin. 'I'm not greedy. The 2C is all Ellen and me can ever handle. And I'd rather see a lot of little farmers fencing off the prairie than one big outfit running beef on the grass.

'It wouldn't take a big outfit long to want to be bigger. Pretty soon they'd find the prairie a little dry come summer and they'd take to running stock where it's greener. That'd mean our valley—mine and Gil Abbey's. It's not generosity—it's just looking out for myself.'

Joel let the reference slide without comment. But in a moment he said. 'We all do things just for ourselves. No matter what tags we hang on them.'

Tim's grin faded, leaving his features strained and sober. 'I can't figure where you're heading,' he said. 'Damn it,' he said into Joel's silence, 'we were friends before we were relatives, Joel. It seems to me I got a right to ask.

'Maybe I don't know, myself,' Joel said quietly. 'But I came in here to start a law office, not fight a war.'

'It isn't your war,' Tim agreed. 'Sure,' he burst out, 'if you can sit it through, you'll be able to start your law office easy when it's over—and no enemies made from fighting on one side or the other, either.' He touched his spurs to his horse and rode head, leaving the bitter words hanging behind him.

Joel kept on the same pace, watching Tim's figure grow smaller as his horse put distance between them. After a few minutes he slowed, but Joel did nothing, and so they rode that way, two hundred yards apart.

Joel had to smile because Tim had not changed. Even as he had what Elmira Reeves called a riding temper, so did Tim have a riding tongue.

'And now it's laid in front of me,' he said, as if to his horse.

He was a lawyer, and a lawyer was a public figure much like a sheriff or a marshal. And no public figure lived without making enemies.

Restlessly, he looked westward, his eyes following the flat plane of the prairie to where it blended into the far hills, their ridgeline tipped with the first sunrise.

Freedom, he thought. Freedom was a precious thing and once a man got his hands on it, he should keep his grip. If he let these people make him choose one side or the other, he would be bound and his freedom gone. Or, like Sam Teel, he could sit it out and let his soul starve, and in the end he would have no enemies.

Angrily he touched his heels to the horse and took after Tim.

They rode on in silence toward the upper end of the valley. Near its narrowing head, the wagon road met the river again and both swung east, going into a small canyon that cut a gap through the hills. The river narrowed suddenly, squeezed between two walls of dark rock. The road followed it along a ledge, making a gentle climb to a summit, so that at the top the river was fifty feet below.

The wind moved through the gap in a soft, steady blowing that filled the air with a curious, low sibilance.

'Whispering Canyon,' Tim said. 'Hear it? The wind never quits here. It comes out of our valley and rolls through here steady.' There was a slight restraint in his voice but at Joel's nod of interest he talked on with the freedom of relief. 'It's a fine pass. The wind keeps most of the snow blowed off the road and—' He paused, looked at Joel, and went on, '—and one man could sit in here and hold back an army if he needed to.'

Joel said nothing. When they broke sharply out of the high-walled cut into the valley the sun was out and he could stretch toward its warmth.

The valley lay spread out, with the sun on the early new grass, a soft green carpet that sloped upward to the east and swung in two horns to the right and left to meet in the distance. The road branched, one fork fording the creek and going north and the other following up the valley south and east.

'Abbey's over there,' Tim said, pointing to the north road. 'His spread is about the same size as mine and he thinks about it the same as

I do. We figure if we don't overgraze, we can make a living for a long time to come. And that's enough for any man to want.

'Of course, since Abbey talked Nora Reeves into marrying him, he's got big dreams. He doesn't think it's enough for her. But he'll get over it after they get married.'

Enough for two here, certainly, Joel agreed.

They rounded a shoulder of hill and came suddenly onto the 2C spread. It was a cluster of log buildings, on a knoll above the creek they had followed. From the house smoke rose straight and high in the clear air, and Joel pushed his horse a little faster, thinking of seeing his sister again.

A horse stood in the yard, ground-reined. Tim Cardon gave a soft grunt when he saw it.

'That's Abbey's horse. What's he doing here so early? He hasn't had time to wind up his chores yet.'

'Maybe,' Joel said, 'he got tired of his own cooking.'

They were in the yard now and Tim rode close to Abbey's sorrel pony. 'A man would have to want food awful bad to ride a horse as fast as this one's been ridden,' he said.

Gil Abbey came from the kitchen before they were well out of the saddle. He was a tall, slender man, his body and walk fitted to the saddle. He had loose blond hair above a finely drawn face, and his eyes, of a color between blue and green, measured a man steadily but without insolence.

He waited until they were by the door before he spoke.

'Keno and a crew came in before daylight,' he said then.

'Cobble?' Tim asked.

'Just Keno and his toughs,' Abbey said. He teetered a little on his bootheels. 'They passed my place just about daybreak.'

'Does Keno want trouble?' Joel asked. He was thinking that Abbey could not have known of last night's fracas so soon.

'You're Lockhart?' Joel nodded and put out his hand to meet Abbey's firm grip. 'Keno usually means trouble,' Abbey answered.

'We had a run-in last night,' Tim said.

They filed inside, Joel going first. He felt the warmth of the large, bright kitchen as he went to greet his sister. He thought her face looked strained as she turned from the stove to give him a welcoming kiss. She was a slender woman, younger than his own thirty years, and short where he was tall, but with the same well-molded flesh over fine bones and the same dark, nearly black hair.

Gil Abbey spoke from behind him. 'I didn't know about the trouble. I was thinking of our stock.'

Ellen Cardon relaxed, gladness on her face at the sight of Tim. 'You were gone a long time,' she said. 'What's this about trouble?'

He ruffled her hair affectionately before he

pulled a chair from the table and sat down. 'I tried to ventilate Abe Cobble, and nobody seemed to like the idea.'

'You had reason enough,' she said.

'Joel helped cool me,' Tim said. He looked toward Joel, his eyes faintly amused. 'He wasn't taking up Cobble's fight or mine, either. He tried to cool Keno later so's to even it up.'

'Maybe Keno came out to see you, then,' Abbey said.

Ellen, with characteristic quick movements that Joel remembered, beat hotcake batter and soon had breakfast on the table. While she worked, she said, 'He didn't come here. And I don't intend to let him come here.'

'You think Keno's rustling your stock?' Joel asked.

'He hires men to do it,' she said.

Gil Abbey took a sip of his coffee and blew his breath at the sudden heat. 'We think,' he said. 'We don't know.'

'I know,' Tim said angrily. 'Clay Harkman owns Keno and he owns Abe Cobble.' He swung his head toward Joel, the violence showing in his face. 'Gil's the kind to believe a man good until he gets a bullet in the brisket. I don't intend to wait that long.'

Ellen set the platter of hotcakes on the table. 'Tim and I worked for this place. It's been five years since we came here. And for two years there wasn't even a store within a day's ride.' She spattered her words at Joel.

'And I won't let a man come in and take away what we've built.'

'Does Harkman want your ranch?'

'He wants what we stand for,' his sister said. 'He wants to wipe out the solid strength of the people who came and settled and intend to stay that way!'

'You don't *know* it's Harkman,' Abbey said quietly.

'Has he bothered the farmers?' Joel asked.

'When he has to, he will,' Ellen answered heatedly. 'But they look to us and to Jed and Elmira for their security. If he can pull down that security, they'll break. Once we go, they'll scatter.'

Tim ate his breakfast with a peculiar viciousness. But when his plate was clean, he pushed back his chair and began to talk.

'They're not just using a long rope on unbranded stuff,' he said. 'They're cutting out thirty, fifty head at a time. By fall we'll be through. Both of us. And that beef isn't going out of the country. There's no place to sell it.'

The silence fell again, and Abbey was the first to speak. 'Tim thinks they're driving the stock into Lost Hole.' Joel made a querying sound, and he went on, 'Some miners found it last year. It's supposed to set east of here, lower than this valley, about twice the size, with grass belly-deep and the snow gone first. I've heard there was a draw leading in, but we've ridden these hills a long time without finding it. The miners left the country and no one else has ever seen anything. It's all talk as far as I can make out.'

'Where else could they go?' Tim demanded. He got to his feet. 'Keno'd be a fool to try and run our beef in broad daylight, but I'm going to see anyway.'

'All right,' Joel said. He stood up, shaping and lighting a cigarette while he waited for Abbey. Ellen was quiet, eating without enthusiasm.

When they were ready to go, she said to Joel, 'I see you wore your gun.'

'Habit,' he said briefly, and turned away from the expression of her eyes.

Outside, the sun had thawed the white frost off the ground. The air had warmed and the riding was more pleasant. They made good time, following the crescent of the mountain to make a complete circle and reach Abbey's before starting again for home.

After they passed the rugged, canyon-cut eastern boundary of the grass, they saw the men from Lace Curtain. Joel was in the lead coming over a rise and they were not fifty yards away from him, off their horses, squatting by the creek bank.

Joel reined in sharply, moving his hand up so that Tim and Abbey followed suit. They sat at the top of the knoll, looking down and studying the group of five. The men did not look up but continued to stare at the creek.

Tim swore under his breath.

'Easy,' Joel said. 'Ride down slow.'

Tim slapped the butt of his carbine and loosened it in its boot. Abbey put a hand out in caution. 'They're not fishing,' he said. 'Don't walk into a trap.'

They rode on, Abbey taking the lead. If it was a trap, then Keno and his men had the trigger fined down, Joel thought. They had risen as if unconcerned at the approaching men and were standing easily while they waited.

Tim's impatience carried him past Abbey in the last ten yards and he wheeled his horse alongside the men and brought it to a sharp stop.

'Looking for beef?'

Keno lifted his long, lantern jawed face without expression. 'Panning a little,' he said shortly.

The men with him Joel recognized as those he had seen last night, plus Seth Markle.

'This is cattle graze,' Tim said.

Keno looked at Abbey. 'It's your range, not Cardon's,' he said. His rumbling voice shut out Tim Cardon.

'There's no color in these creeks,' Abbey told him.

Seth Markle spat on the ground. 'I got color,' he said. He swung his head and Joel looked toward the creek where a gold pan rested on the bank. He got off his horse, handing the reins to Tim, and walked to the pan.

Stooping, he looked into the bits of gravel and fine sand, and probing, he saw the color. It was rich. He studied the creek and followed its eastward wandering with his eyes. There was a wrongness here he could not identify, and so he pushed it to the back of his mind and turned to the others.

'It's heavy,' he said.

Keno smiled insolently at Abbey and Tim Cardon. 'It was cattle graze,' he said, 'but by the time the news gets around, it won't be.' He waved a hand at his men. 'Stake your claims and let's get home.'

'There'll be no claims staked in this valley,' Abbey said. His voice was slow and calm, but the power of it turned Keno toward him. The flat surfaces of his eyes showed nothing as they probed at Abbey.

'No?' His deep voice held an indefinable softness. 'You mean there won't be nothing *but* claims here.'

Tim Cardon wheeled his horse and brought up his carbine. 'This is private land, Keno. Now high-tail.' He jerked his head toward their horses picketed near by. 'Any man caught panning on this creek answers to us. Tell that to Clay Harkman.'

Joel stepped forward quickly. 'Put that gun down, Tim,' he said. His voice was quiet but it held a carrying sharpness. 'You,' he said to

Keno, 'ride out of here. We'll let the courts decide that.'

'Making business for yourself, lawyer?'

'Keeping business from the undertaker,' Joel said.

'It wouldn't stop a rush if Cardon shot us,' Keno rumbled reasonably. 'He can't shoot every miner that wants to come in here.' He laughed. 'There ain't that much lead and powder around.'

'There's enough for you,' Tim said.

Abbey rode alongside him and clamped a quick hand over his gun. 'Not yet,' he said. 'Lockhart's right.'

'You think a court'll stop 'em any faster'n bullets?' Tim cried.

There was a silent struggle with Abbey not loosening his grip on the gun and Tim not willing to lose his advantage. Keno's crew still stood, making no effort to reach their own guns, apparently as uninterested in the outcome of this as men without a stake in it.

Joel felt the wrongness of it again, more strongly this time. It was unnatural for men like these to stand aside when riches lay at their feet. *They have their orders,* he thought. Keno obviously kept them in line, and just as obviously Keno could let them loose.

Once more Joel spoke. 'Ease down, Tim. And you men move out. This gold isn't getting up and walking away.'

'I'm filing,' Seth Markle said. He began a

swaggering walk toward the creek.

Keno's voice lashed out, halting him. 'Not now. Lockhart's right. The gold ain't walking off. We'll go—for now.'

'And let *them* file?' Markle said. He looked at Joel, his lips pulled back over broken teeth.

'Preventing us from filing with that gun is the same as claim jumping,' Keno said. 'We can wait.'

He walked away, his long stride carrying him toward the horses. The others followed, Markle going last, looking at Joel a long while before he left.

When they were out of sight Tim swore violently. 'I had 'em,' he said. 'What's the matter with you two?'

'You'd just start an open war,' Joel said. 'Are you prepared for one?'

'I am,' Tim said.

'No,' Abbey said with more caution. 'It would be about a hundred to ten if it came to a showdown.'

Joel nodded. 'Another way,' he said, and bent to the creek again. He lifted his head after a moment. 'Did anybody ever pan these creeks?'

'Last year,' Abbey said. 'There's no color.'

'Never was!' Tim cried out. 'They're running one on us, Joel. The headwaters up on the slope don't carry gold, either. These aren't gold-bearing sands. Markle planted that dust in the pan.'

'I saw that,' Joel said. 'But before you can prove it to the miners, they'll be in here so thick the United States Cavalry won't be able to keep them out. I know miners. Once the news gets around, there won't be room in this valley for your beef.'

They rode back quickly, stopping at Abbey's house and leaving him there. 'I'll come over and ride back to town with you,' he told Joel, and reined his horse toward the corral.

Tim led the way to his place, setting a fast pace.

Ellen was waiting quietly, dinner on the table, some of it growing cold. She started for Tim, but stopped, hiding her concern when she saw the hot anger in him.

Joel told the story briefly and when he was done she said only, 'I'll not have it. There won't be any miners setting foot on 2C grass.'

'The news'll be all over the Territory in a week,' Tim said. 'I could have bottled it up right here if Joel and Abbey hadn't been so damned quick with the law.'

'Killing six men not fighting back is no way,' Joel said. 'And it would only bring sixty more.'

Tim jerked out his chair and flung himself into it.

'This is another of Harkman's plans,' Ellen said. 'How can we stop it?'

'No way,' Joel told her. 'Even if you owned the mineral rights to your own homesteads, miners could come in and stake the rest of the range.'

He hated to see the look of bitter defeat touching his sister's eyes. She seated herself, motioning for Joel to do likewise. 'We want your help,' she said. 'This will go against Elmira and Jed, and the farmers as well as us, and together we might be able to do something.'

'Get together, then. You don't need me for that.'

'We're country and they're town,' Ellen said. 'We're friends but we don't all see things the same way.'

'Harkman holds his side together tight enough,' Tim burst out. 'We can't lick him until we do the same.'

'If it's Harkman,' Joel said, echoing Abbey. He bent his head and began to eat.

CHAPTER FIVE

Before supper he rode back to town. Abbey went with him, and they remained silent until they had broken out of the valley and turned south toward town.

Abbey spoke at last. 'It's hard to think of losing a place you've built up,' he said. 'And I had it going good for Nora just before the rustling started. And now this—' He broke off. 'It won't leave much to offer her,' he added.

Joel remembered the quiet, clear-eyed girl he had met the night before. 'She won't be one to ask more than her share,' he said.

'That doesn't stop a man from wanting to give it to her,' Abbey answered. 'Now, there won't even be that.' He rode on again, silent, until dissatisfaction broke through his mood. 'But if we're licked, we're licked, that's all. There're too many of them.'

Joel made no answer. He was thinking of what his sister had asked him—to come in and take their feelings for his own and fight for them. They all had their own goals and they thought by working together each one could reach his particular one.

'I'll see Harkman,' he decided.

In town, he left Abbey by Reeves' store and continued on to Teel's, where he turned over the horse. He went to the glowing forge to warm himself before going back to the street.

Teel turned his cautious blue eyes on him. 'You find things peaceable?'

Joel pointed to a broken plowshare near the forge. 'You'd do better to hammer a few swords out of that,' he said, and walked out.

He hesitated, trying to decide whether to go into the hotel dining room or to Harkman's saloon to eat. He chose the latter, knowing that the way a man's business was run often told something of the man himself.

Inside the wide saloon doors it was warm, the cold pushed out by the smell of men and stale whiskey and tobacco smoke that hung in blue layers on the air. There were no more than a dozen men inside, some lined along the bar and some at the gambling tables in the rear.

Keno was not in sight, nor were any of the men who had been with him at the creek. Joel was puzzled by the quiet in the saloon. If the news of a gold strike, no matter how faked, had been let out, there would be excitement here. The quiet meant but one thing: for reasons of his own, Keno was keeping the news back.

Turning to the bar, he saw a man taller than Keno, and one who looked as if he could be twice as dangerous. Joel decided this must be the Leppy Gotch he had been told of—the man who could find it in him to love Seth Markle. He was a huge man, with the lumbering bulk of a buffalo. His face was gross, but lacking the fat of Abe Cobble. When his gaze came to Joel the vacancy in his eyes was plain.

Joel walked to the bar.

'Supper?'

The big man pointed to the lunch counter where food steamed into the thick air. 'Dollar,' he said, 'and beer.' Joel bought the beer and took it across the empty dance floor to a table. Returning he scooped food onto a plate, piling potatoes and beans on a thick slice of beef and starting carefully back across the floor.

The door swung open, letting in cold air, and he glanced over to see Seth Markle stamping his feet and looking about. He was showing his liquor, a man looking for trouble and hoping he would find it.

He saw Joel and started across the floor. Joel went on at the same pace, balancing the plateful of food. When Markle was at Joel's back he seemed to stumble, and an elbow caught Joel's arm where it crooked. Joel stumbled and the plate slipped to the floor.

It turned in the air and landed face down, the food making a squashing sound as it splayed out from under the pressure of the plate.

The clinking of chips and the riffling of cards faded out. The one sound was the expectant breathing of the watchers. The big man behind the bar was motionless, his hand holding an empty beer glass in the air. The men along the bar were half turned to face the dance floor.

Joel's stumble had carried him around so that he faced Markle. His head bent as he looked down at the shorter man. Markle was breathing heavily and he let a small, mean grin of anticipation crawl around his mouth as he waited.

Joel was the first to speak. 'Lick it up,' he said. His voice was steady with the cold, dominating rage that had come over him.

Markle made a laughing sound and belched.

He swung away, taking one contemptuous step before Joel's hand caught his shoulder and spun him back. He threw up his arms but Joel batted them aside and slapped him, rocking his head back and forth a half-dozen times before he could block the blows.

Markle made a blubbering sound and lowered his head. He charged in, bull-like, and Joel stepped aside. His anger fined him, giving him the advantage over Markle's whiskey-red rage. He thrust out a foot as Markle stumbled, tripping the man and cascading him to the floor to slide along its polished surface on his face.

Joel brought him to his knees with a grip on his collar. Markle turned, but Joel caught an arm and levered it up his back, halting his motion with the pressure.

'Get it over with,' Joel said softly. He brought Markle's arm up higher and twisted. him toward the plate of spilled food.

Markle walked to it on his knees, head down, his breath coming through his open mouth. His every motion was a protest but under the pressure on his arm he went.

'Lick it up,' Joel said again. 'Lick it clean, Markle.'

Markle held out a moment longer, his neck muscles rigid with strain. But the pain was telling, rolling the sweat out on his face. He tried to rear up, his head high, and he stayed that way briefly, as if ready to struggle to his feet against the strength of Joel's hammer lock.

Then Markle's head went down and his body bent. Mouth open and tongue out, he reached for the food.

A long-drawn sigh vibrated through the room, and Joel lifted his head. Still no one moved and laughter from a card player in the rear gurgled back in the man's throat.

Markle made a retching sound but the strength of Joel's grip held him down. When Joel released his grip and straightened up, Markle made a move to crawl away, but Joel brought a foot against his neck, holding him.

At last it was done and Joel took his foot away. He stepped to one side, facing the bar. 'Get up.'

Markle stumbled to his feet, shaking his head to clear it. He turned twice to get his bearings and then aimed himself at the doors and flung himself out of sight into the night.

Someone guffawed and the rest took it up until the sound beat loudly in the low-ceilinged room. Behind the bar Leppy Gotch stood like stone, a glass squeezed in his hand. His heavy face was twisted with anguish, but he did not move.

Joel went to the bar and saw that the man next to him held a gun flat on the bar surface. It was the same man who had stepped from the saloon to light has pipe the night before, the man who had been waiting by the saloon corner later, backing Jed Hopper.

'Draw me a beer before you bust that glass, Leppy,' he said. Without looking at Joel, he spoke to him. 'Leppy here didn't like it.'

Leppy Gotch swung his huge head toward Joel. Hatred blurred his vacant eyes. 'Markle ain't going to like it, neither,' he said in a whimpering voice. 'We'll do something about it, too.'

Joel filled a second plate with food and carried it to his table, seated himself and began to eat.

The man who had demanded the beer got it and walked across the room to Joel. He stood before him with his solid squatness of strength, legs as bowed as the hoop of a barrel. His face was clean under a trimmed spade beard that was going gray in the red, and there was a humorous quirk to his heavy mouth.

'Thanks for the help,' Joel said.

'It wasn't enough,' Abel Kine said. He pulled out a chair and sat down. 'After that, I aim to rest. You don't seem worried none.' He had a slow, amiable voice.

'What's done is done,' Joel said. He shook his head. 'Fight gets in a man and he doesn't always take the most sensible way.'

'If you'd thought it out you would'a done the same thing,' Kine said. 'You got that look about you.'

Joel bent to eating again. When he was through and nothing more had been said, he finished his beer and began a slow shaping of a cigarette. 'Get to the point,' he said.

'I'm Kine,' the man told him. 'Abel Kine. Hardrock.'

'This is placer country,' Joel said.

The humor on Abel Kine's mouth switched to contempt. 'Placer! Piddling placer. Hardrock's where the mother lode lies. I was hardrock in Californy and I'm hardrock here.'

Joel smoked placidly, waiting for Kine to say what he had come for. No man pulled out his gun to help a stranger unless there was a reason back of it. And this miner had the look of a man who knew his way about.

'I liked the way you handled yourself, last night,' he said. 'I asked around some about you and I liked what I heard, too.' Beneath his mild voice Joel could detect a current of roughness. 'I might need some help,' Kine went on.

Joel was very still, wondering if he were being given another reason to stay. 'Elmira Reeves send you to me?'

The answer was in Kine's amazement. Joel nodded, smiling a little to himself.

'What kind of help?' he asked.

Kine finished his beer at one gulp and set down the glass. 'I heard talk of another placer rush,' he said.

'Then the news is out?'

'No,' Kine said. 'I got it from Jed through Abbey.' Abbey had spread it fast, Joel thought, and looked again at Kine. He went on, 'A placer rush means they'll be all over my claim.'

'And you want a lawyer to protect you?'

'Lawyer, hell!' Kine said. 'I want to stop them before they get here. I—' He broke off, staring toward the rear of the saloon. 'You got company,' he said.

He stood up and moved away, as if the man approaching were something with which he did not want to be tainted. It was Keno.

'I hear I got my floor mopped.'

Joel put both hands against the edge of the table and pushed back his chair. Keno raised a hand. 'No more trouble,' he said in his gravelled tones. 'Harkman wants to see you.'

'My office will be in the hotel,' Joel said. 'If I set up an office.'

Keno regarded Joel from his long, somber face, his narrow black eyes veiled, holding back whatever he was thinking. 'You're a touchy man,' he said. 'This ain't my business. I'm just bringing a message. Harkman's *asking.* You want he should write you a letter?'

'All right,' Joel said. He got up and followed Keno the length of the room to the stairs and up them. At the top Keno pointed down the hall to the front and Joel went that way.

He did not knock. Hand lifted, he held it, calling out, 'Harkman?'

There was a quick sound and the door came open. Clay Harkman smiled as he stepped back, holding the door. Joel could feel the impact of his charm and smoothness. Crossing the room, he took a chair by Harkman's desk. Harkman went around and sat behind it.

Joel looked about, studying the wood-paneled walls, the thick fur rugs on the floor, the fireplace with a big log burning warmly. He felt the permanence of the room and of the man in it.

'I saw the affair from the foot of the stairs,' Harkman said. He pushed an open cigar box toward Joel.

Taking one of Harkman's thin, fragrant cigars, Joel accepted a light. 'So?'

'So you choose sides quickly, Lockhart.'

'I've chosen no side,' Joel said irritably. 'All I've heard is sides. Had it been Sam Teel or Jed Hopper or you, I would have done the same thing.'

'Your trigger's quick,' Harkman remarked. 'All right, I'm wrong. But you've heard them damn me?'

'I've heard talk,' Joel said.

'What I want,' Harkman said with bluntness, 'is a rich town here. A strong town so we can get a county.'

'So does Elmira Reeves,' Joel said.

'And to call it Lace Curtain!' Harkman made a brushing gesture with his hand. 'A town for old women.' He stopped, and laughed softly. 'But that is neither here nor there. Call it what you will, the result should be the same.'

He took time to light a cigar for himself and

when it was drawing well he stared across the desk, not at Joel but at something beyond.

'What have your plans to do with me?'

Harkman brought Joel's face into focus with his eyes. 'You didn't come here without a reason.'

'My sister lives here,' Joel said.

Harkman made the brushing motion with his hand again. 'That has no meaning.' He leaned forward and the intensity of his words was reflected in his face. 'You're a lawyer, Lockhart. What does a lawyer want? To help make the laws. Of his county, of his territory, eventually of his state.' He held up a hand, crushing air in strong fingers. 'He is the molder of society.'

'I've thought all those things,' Joel admitted. 'Every man has thought them.'

Harkman leaned back, breathing deeply. 'Then I'm wasting my words. I need only invite you to join me. This is rich country, Lockhart. It's a good framework on which to build.'

'I haven't made up my mind to stay or go.'

'Good, good,' Harkman said. His heavy mouth creased in a smile. 'But if you stay—the offer lies open.'

Joel rose, laying down the cigar. 'To join you? And Keno?'

'Keno?' Harkman's thick eyebrows went up. 'He runs my saloon. That's all.'

'I've heard otherwise,' Joel said.

'As I said you would,' Harkman agreed. He

spoke softly. 'I make no claims, one way or the other. The choice is yours, Lockhart.'

Joel thought. *This man is clever,* and turned it aside. 'I've been told Seth Markle didn't like what I did. So I may have no choice.'

Harkman's eyes were fixed on him. 'If you're afraid—?' He took a gun from his desk and made a move to hand it to Joel.

Joel walked to the door and went out.

He walked down the stairs and to the front doors. Men were talking again but they grew silent as he came into view.

Joel put a hand against the batwings and pushed. The cold air gushed in at him and the darkness of night was blinding after the strong lights inside. He heard the silence behind him and he stepped to the board sidewalk.

'This is a fool thing,' he murmured to himself. He should have accepted Harkman's loan of a gun. When he stepped into a shadow past the edge of the saloon the darkness was complete.

The click of the gun hammer warned him and he threw himself to one side. Flame gushed into the night and the sound of the bullet slapping board by his feet was a sudden sound.

Markle, he thought, had found the range soon enough.

CHAPTER SIX

A second patch of shadow lay against the darkened side of the saloon. Joel dropped to the sidewalk and rolled.

Off the sidewalk and in darkness, he rose to a crouch, waiting. There was a scraping sound as the man by the building tried to get a better sight for his shooting. Joel felt in the dirt and put his fingers around a small, sharp rock. He twisted, still in the crouch, and with one motion flung the rock at the wall of the saloon and leaped sideways.

The sound of the rock striking wood came almost with the crash of the gun. Dust spurted where the bullet hit dirt, but Joel was to one side, moving in.

He came up against the man, hip to hip, his hands reaching for the gun arm. By the man's breath he knew it was Seth Markle. There was a grunting sound as Joel's fingers closed on a thick wrist. He lay back, dragging Markle over one leg.

'Drop it!'

Markle swore at him until his breath was almost gone. He lashed at Joel's groin with his free arm and Joel turned the blow with a raised knee.

Markle was fighting now with more strength than he had shown in the saloon, and with a wrench he straightened and pinned Joel to the saloon wall. They hung that way. Markle straining to get his gun arm free and his weight holding Joel from throwing him.

Soft footsteps came up to them and a dark shape merged with the shadow. Markle made a noise, and a voice said:

'Let loose of that gun, Markle.

The gun made a thudding sound as it hit the dirt and Markle swore again. The man in front of them bent and then faded back, past their range of vision.

'You're even now,' he said.

Joel let loose of Markle's wrist. Markle jumped to one side, swinging. Joel brought the open edge of his palm against the swinging arm and Markle cried out in pain. Joel ducked in and drummed two short, sharp blows to Markle's heart. Markle gave ground and Joel hit him again.

Now Markle swung with his other arm but Joel was out of reach. He came in again, batting Markle's one-handed swings aside. With the steady precision of a man performing an operation, he began to batter Markle's face.

'No more,' Markle gasped, and Joel stopped.

'Bully someone else,' he said in a quiet tone. 'After this, leave me alone, do you hear?'

There was no answer and he roweled his hip into Markle's body. 'I hear,' Markle said.

Joel stepped back, letting Markle come free of the wall. He took a wobbly step forward and

Joel hit him with his fist. He caught Markle flush on the side of the jaw so that he stumbled and then dropped. He rolled once, half out of the shadow into the light, and lay still.

Joel turned, tired from his own efforts.

He remembered the deliberate way he had let Markle free, only to batter him down again. *Am I cruel*? he thought.

Abel Kine appeared at his side. 'You sure ain't making a friend of him,' he said.

Joel answered both Kine and himself. 'It's the only language he knows. The fear of God needs to be in him.'

'No,' Kine said. 'It's useless. He's the kind who's brave with a gun in his hand. And nothing short of a bullet in the brisket will stop him from trying it again.'

Joel walked on, until he came to the hotel. He turned into the lobby with Kine following him. Jed Hopper spoke to them from his position behind the rough counter.

'Heard you roughed up Markle some,' he said.

'For the second time,' Kine told him. 'I went out to see he got a fair shake, but he was doing all right.'

Joel heard Kine out and then shook his head. 'He still had his gun when you came along.'

Hopper said, 'No matter. It's still no good, Lockhart. It's no more good than trying to change a rock wall from being what it is by dynamiting it.'

'Then,' Joel said, 'I can only keep dynamiting —until there's nothing left but the rubble.'

*   *   *

Abbey, leaving Joel, turned his horse toward the Reeves house. He found supper waiting and he washed up and took his seat. His grave countenance showed his hunger for Nora as he bent to catch her words.

'Did you see the new man?' she was asking him.

'I saw him,' Abbey said. He spooned potatoes onto his plate, set down the potato dish and looked at Elmira Reeves. 'He thinks you're trying to argue him into staying.'

'I am,' she said brusquely. 'I want him here. I can use a man like that.'

'How do we know?' Abbey demanded. 'Maybe we see in him what we want to see, and he isn't that at all.'

'There are stories,' Nora said. 'And a feeling about him—' She felt Abbey's eyes on her and she gave him an amused smile. 'For the town, Gil, not for me.'

He flushed at having been caught so easily. 'I still say, wait and see.'

'We've waited,' Elmira said tartly. She helped herself to food and began to eat. 'We've waited and there isn't much more time.'

'You can't rope him like a steer,' Abbey said.

'There's a way,' Elmira answered. 'I'm offering it to Harkman tonight.' Her determination was in her voice. 'Some of the farmers will be in, too.'

'Are you starting something you can't finish, Elmira?'

'I can't finish it alone,' she said, her voice sharp with implication.

Abbey busied himself with eating. Feeling the eyes of both women on him, he sighed and raised his head. 'I'll help,' he said. 'If it comes to it, I'll help.'

'You can start right after supper,' Elmira said, 'by getting Harkman over here. Tell him there's a meeting it's to his advantage to attend.'

'All right,' Abbey said.

After he had gone, Elmira Reeves began to carry dishes to the kitchen. Nora rose to help. 'You're rough on Gil,' she said.

Elmira made a snorting sound. 'He's weak. There's something about the man—' She shook her head. 'We can't use weakness.'

'You mistake gentleness for weakness,' Nora said. 'Gil is a quiet man, Mother. He dreams of big things.'

'Dreams? What use are dreams?'

'I like them,' Nora said simply, 'when they're for me.'

She continued her work quietly, not speaking. Was it weakness, she wondered? But she had felt it, too. Still, she hugged the thought of his dreams to her.

'I'm really less desiring than he thinks,' she said to herself. But it was his nature to expect her to want many things, and lately she had not tried to convince him otherwise.

What do I want? she wondered. What did any woman want beyond peace and the growth of herself and her surroundings in which she lived? Children, perhaps, and the knowledge that they would be raised in a better world than she had known.

These things Abbey could give her. He was a man without restlessness. He was willing to stay where he was and build on what he had. If only he would be satisfied to build to his limits, and not strive to go beyond them. Life could be simple if he would let it be so.

'He dreams big things,' she said again to her mother.

'Dreams don't find rustled cattle,' Elmira answered.

* * *

Abbey went to Harkman's office by way of the rear stairs. He stood at the top of the stairs, in darkness, for some time before he was sure the hallway was empty. Then he opened the door and walked slowly down the hall.

What was the use, he thought, of bucking things? Elmira was wasting strength she could turn to other uses. With the spring, miners were bound to pour in, wanting food and supplies. And she could take their gold instead of sending it elsewhere.

He thought of the dust that had been measured over store counters during last summer's rush. Dust to stock ten thousand acres and hire a crew to work them. He knew the big house he wanted to build and the fine things he could get to fill it. Rich silks for Nora and a maid to dress her in them. A mahogany table to eat at and the best china to put on it.

His eyes shone with the glitter of the dream and he stopped to break free from it before he raised his hands and knocked on Harkman's door.

A voice said, 'Come,' and Abbey stepped in, closing the door.

Harkman, behind his desk, motioned for Abbey to sit.

'It seems Lockhart roughed Markle up some tonight.' He told the story while Abbey listened in silence.

'So,' Abbey said, 'Lockhart chose his side.'

'So I thought,' Harkman said. 'But Lockhart claims not.' He spread his hands in a shrug. 'He's a hard man to judge.'

'Elmira plans to keep him here and use him,' Abbey said.

Harkman's eyes were small and hidden

behind the mask of his face. 'You were a fool if you came here to tell me that.'

Abbey rolled a cigarette and lighted it. 'She sent me over to bring you for a meeting. With the farmers.'

'Ah,' Harkman said, 'she's afraid to wait any longer. What's the meeting for?'

Abbey's voice was dry. 'You're to help keep Lockhart here, I gather.'

'For her purposes?'

'It would seem so.'

Harkman laughed. 'I'll go.'

Abbey rolled his cigarette slowly between his thumb and finger, feeling the dry tobacco rustle.

'I don't like Keno and his crew on my creek,' he said. He looked squarely at Harkman. 'I don't like the idea of a gold rush on good beef grass.'

'It might not come to that,' Harkman assured him. 'If Cardon bluffs out, the news won't be spread.'

'Cardon won't bluff out,' Abbey said. 'He'll stand at the pass with a rifle.' He paused and stared down at the cigarette he had crumpled. 'And so will I,' he added softly. 'I won't let my graze be ruined.'

Harkman smiled with his mouth, his head shaking slowly. 'A shortsighted man isn't a smart man, Abbey. What's a few acres of grass now, compared to a few thousand later?' Shrewdly, he waited, and then dropped his words one by one into Abbey's mind, slowly so that none of them would be lost.

'There's a whole valley here for a cattleman to have. There are mountainsides for summer grass, too. A lot of land for one man. It will make a lot of beef.'

Abbey thought of the fine house and the mahogany and china, the paintings on the walls and soft rugs on the floor. He breathed deeply. With a sudden angry motion he flung his cigarette at a spittoon.

'I don't like it,' he said. 'I built my place from nothing. So did Tim. And to let a bunch of miners come in and take over—'

Harkman interrupted, 'A weak man gets nothing, Abbey.' His voice took on a faint sneer. 'You know what you have now. You know what you can have—soon. But if you're too weak, too soft to take a chance for it . . . He let his words trail off.

Abbey bowed his head, staring at the pattern of the floor but not seeing it. When he raised his face his eyes were blank, indrawn. 'All right, Harkman. But don't turn the miners loose unless you have to. Don't spread the news until there's nothing else to do.'

'I never play my hole card at the beginning of a game,' Harkman said.

* * *

Joel smoked and drank Jed Hopper's coffee as

he watched the farmers file into the kitchen, one after the other. They were men of a pattern, clean and neat in patched overalls, their hands hard and gnarled from gripping plow handles. They stood in silence until they were all together and then went out with Hopper and Abel Kine.

Joel saw now what Elmira Reeves had meant. These were the solid men, the men who would put into the land, not take out of it. They represented permanence and quiet but never-ending resistance to the things Clay Harkman was supposed to want. He felt their strength as they stood together behind Jed Hopper. But alone they were nothing; plows without a guiding hand, cutting crazy furrows across a field. They were the kind who had been driven too often from their homesteads to think they could fight alone.

He drained the coffee pot and stood restlessly. He went into the lobby and through it to the street. It was empty and dark and there was no sound but the distant tinkle of the saloon piano.

He turned back into the lobby, his tiredness gone under a strong urge to find his solution and do one thing or the other: choose his side and stay, or pack his trunk and leave.

He was startled when he saw Nora Reeves coming from the kitchen to the hotel desk. 'I thought,' he said, 'there was a meeting at your house.'

'One vote to a family,' she said. 'And someone has to watch the hotel.'

'So much business,' he said, and laughed with her.

'I heard about Seth Markle,' she said. 'From Gil.'

'You don't approve?' he asked. He studied her thoughtful expression, heightened by the lamplight.

'Are you always so cruel?'

'Cruel? I could have accepted Markle's cruelty,' he said. 'And I would have been subjected to it as long as I stayed here.' He added with shrewdness, 'Abbey is a quiet man but he would never have taken it.'

'Perhaps not, but would he have done so—so much?'

Because he saw he was making her uncomfortable, he changed the subject quickly.

'Abbey has some fine things planned for the future.'

'Gil dreams,' she said, adding a soft smile, 'I want so little and he wants so much for me.'

'As I told him,' Joel said. 'But let him dream. Let him paint his picture with you in the center.'

She was regarding him somberly, thinking that here was a man who had shaped dreams and seen them fail, and had shaped them anew.

'You have a dream?'

'A dream—a vision, no. A goal, yes. The same goal as your mother and Clay Harkman, perhaps.'

She studied him impassively. 'Your wish to reach a goal can't be very strong. If there's effort involved, what do you do—turn aside and look for another one?'

'It's just that I want to make up my own mind,' he said slowly. 'For myself.'

'What of your sister and Tim? Didn't they ask for your help?'

'It's being pushed,' he tried to explain. 'If a man is directed by others, then he has lost his freedom of thought. Then—'

'Freedom of thought!' she broke in. Her voice was a cutting knife of scorn. 'And while you save your precious freedom, others are losing theirs—and all other freedoms as well!' She stopped and the quick anger drained from her eyes, leaving them quietly gray again.

'I'm sorry,' she said. She placed her fingers on his arm. 'It's not my business to say these things to you.'

Before Joel could answer her, the kitchen door swung and Lem Happy came with long strides into the room. 'Jed! Jed, I heard—' He stopped, catching sight of them.

'Jed's at my house for a meeting,' Nora said.

The old man shifted his stringy body in his excitement. 'I can't say it to this fellow,' he said, nodding toward Joel. 'He ain't with us.'

Joel walked across the room to the door.

The street was quiet except for the piano carrying on its steady, empty tinkling. Behind Joel, Lem Happy was muttering. After it ceased, Nora's voice came clearly:

'Go tell Jed, Lem. Go over to the house. But be careful. Harkman is there.'

Joel returned to the desk as Lem Happy went out. He saw the concern on her face and misread it. 'Don't apologize.'

A faint flush touched her cheeks. 'I had no intention of it,' she said. 'But I do intend to tell you. Perhaps you'll do something. Abe Cobble is going to arrest Tim,' she said. 'Trick him into town and then arrest him.'

'Tomorrow or tonight?'

'Tomorrow,' she said. 'The trick will be to cut some cattle from his herd and let him trail them this way. It may start before morning.'

'Whose plan was this?'

'Lem heard Keno telling Seth Markle and Abe Cobble about it,' she said. 'Trick him into town and then arrest him.'

'Tomorrow or tonight?'

'If Tim is warned,' he said, 'there is no need to worry. It's a poor plan at best.'

'That isn't enough!' she cried. 'He needs help, too. Lem will tell Jed and he and the farmers will wrangle as to the best way and by the time they decide—everything will be over.'

Joel said, 'Thank you for telling me,' and went upstairs. He came down in a few minutes, buckling his gun belt around his waist.

'I'm going to see Keno and Cobble,' he told her.

'To tell them we know?' she asked scathingly.

'To make a deal,' he said. He went on out the door.

'You fool!' she cried, and ran out through the kitchen to her own house.

He was across the street and starting for the saloon when a man ran out from between two of the abandoned buildings and spun him around. The man grunted and caught his balance. Light from the hotel windows gleamed on the barrel of a rifle.

'Easy, friend,' Joel said. He recognized the long-trunked man Keno had called Wolf.

Wolf had the rifle leveled at Joel's middle. 'Back where you came from,' he said flatly. 'This ain't no time to take a stroll.'

Joel said, 'I feel like a stroll,' and tried to push the rifle barrel to one side. Wolf stepped back, out of his reach, but the rifle remained steady. Joel shrugged, turned and crossed the street again and went into the lobby.

He was angry, not at Wolf who was probably following someone's orders, but at himself for having backed down so quickly. It went against his grain, irritating him.

He heard voices and footsteps in the kitchen and he went that way. Jed Hopper was there with Kine. Hopper looked sourly at him.

'Thought you went to chin with Keno?'

'Wolf stopped me,' Joel said. 'With a gun.'

'Lem was right,' Hopper said. 'They did see him and they're out after his hide.'

'Lem can take care of himself,' Kine said. He loosened the gun in his holster. 'But I still think I'll take a look around.'

Joel watched him slip out the rear door. 'Is this supposed to be Harkman's doing, too?' he asked. 'Making the plan to get Tim and sending men after Happy?'

'Harkman was with us most of the evening,' Hopper said reluctantly. 'It's more like Keno throwing his weight around.' Joel nodded and started for the front. 'Where you going now?' Hopper demanded.

Joel looked back at him. 'To make two deals with Keno,' he said. 'And take a stroll.'

CHAPTER SEVEN

Clay Harkman returned to his office with the slow walk of a man deep in his thoughts. He paused inside the door, and then swung around as someone came down the hall.

It was Keno. 'We caught that Lem Happy listening,' he said. 'He got away but I sent men out to find him.'

'So that's what the excitement was about,' Harkman said. He stared coldly at Keno. 'You're a fool. Call your men off.'

'But he heard the plan.'

'Then,' Harkman said, 'We'll make a new one. And leave Happy alone for now. We may want him to hear a plan sometime.'

Keno stared at him and then his mouth twisted into a sly grin. 'So we might,' he said, and walked off.

Harkman grunted his disgust and went into his office. He sat down behind the desk and drew a sheet of paper forward. With a fresh pen he began to write, his hand moving with a steady slowness.

A noise from the door of his bedroom drew his head up. He rose when he saw Juanita and beckoned her toward him. He went to the hall door, throwing over the bolt, and then came back to her.

She stood quietly before Harkman, her chiseled features without expression. Only her dark eyes moved, going about the room and coming to rest on his face.

She allowed him to kiss her briefly. 'I've been waiting,' she said. 'It was hard to get out. But there was a minute when the lobby was clear.'

His nod interrupted her and he went to his desk, resuming his chair. 'Be as careful when you leave,' he said. He placed a finger on the paper before him. 'You're the schoolteacher.'

'That's why I came,' she said.

'Elmira Reeves,' he said, nodding in the direction of the street, 'had different ideas.'

His mouth quirked with amusement. ‘She wanted Lockhart to teach school.’ He continued to look at the paper, rather than at her. ‘She didn’t want you.’

She stepped forward, tall and graceful in her movements. ‘Why is this, Clay?’

Somewhere since she had last seen him, he had changed. She studied it, seeking the answer. And when he did raise his head, letting her see his expression, she understood. As his note had said, ‘This time it cannot fail,’ so did his face. It frightened her, this new determination.

‘Nothing,’ she thought, ‘will stop him.’ She had seen his ruthlessness before, and she had dreaded the time when his desire would become this strong.

‘Why is this?’ she asked again.

‘They connect you with me,’ he said simply. ‘But I convinced them it was through a friend.’ He smiled again with the same thinness. ‘I pointed out that you were an experienced schoolteacher. I disclaimed any other knowledge of you. I won out.’

‘Was it worth an argument to have me here?’

He only shrugged but by his expression she knew he was still afraid of her. It was something she had always sensed, but never before had put into her thoughts so plainly. He might be afraid of what she would do, but she was sure it was more. He might find a time when he had need of her. And so it was worth a great deal to have her near, to fill that need should it arise. But this did not warm her as it had before. She felt a strange emptiness, as if he were just another person and no longer mattered.

'My need is gone,' she told herself in surprise. And she could not help but wonder how long his need for her would last.

'Ten years now, Clay, and we've spent more time apart than together. How much longer do I come to you as a stranger?'

'No more,' he said abruptly. 'This is the last time.'

He rose with a rough movement and came around the desk to stand before her. She was nearly as tall as he, but his bulk overwhelmed her. 'I've waited a long time for this opportunity, Juanita. And now is my chance.'

'And so I stay away, in a hotel, waiting again?'

'Later I can court you,' he said. He offered her his charming smile. 'I've done that before.'

'You always were gallant, Clay. But even a woman gets tired of being courted.'

'The last time,' he said. 'Once this has worked out—' He broke off, waving a hand. 'My dear, this is the end of the old and the beginning of the new. I'll grow here, become strong—and you with me. Perhaps you'll help me rule a state!'

'Why must I want such things, Clay?

Because you do? I've followed you from east to west, from south to the north. Always it has been looking for this last place—and each camp was the one.' She shook her head. 'You crush people, Clay, as you've crushed me. And still you never get what you want.'

'I'm getting it now,' he said roughly.

'But if you don't? If this fails?'

She watched him closely, knowing his weaknesses and yet recognizing they were what had held her to him. If he became so strong, she would go—romance had become ashes long ago. Only her protectiveness was left. And in this new strangeness of his, she saw the end of that, the end of herself as a part of him.

'It can't fail,' he said. 'But if it does—if it could—I have other plans.' He stabbed his finger toward the paper on his desk. 'I won't be stopped this time.'

'Someday,' she said, 'your trampling will fail. And before you can run out in the night. Someday it will get you a bullet in the back.'

The lash of her voice brought him forward so that he caught her by the shoulders, but without gentleness. 'Don't talk of those things. They're past—done. And you'll help. That's why we stay strangers—so you can be over there, helping.'

She bit her lip under the pressure of his fingers on her shoulders. 'You're hurting me,' she said. When he dropped his hands, she moved away. 'I'll do as you say—again. But not if you use force. Then I'm through, Clay.'

'Force!'

'I heard some men discuss cattle rustling,' she said.

'That isn't force,' he said. 'When the ranchers are ready to do as I want and go, they can have their cattle back.'

'I heard, too,' she said, 'that Joel Lockhart refuses to join them or you. And I know what this man Markle tried to do to him.'

'I've stopped Markle,' he said. 'And Lockhart will join me. I blocked their move to get him on their side—as a schoolteacher.'

'He wouldn't have taken it,' she said. She thought back to his remark in the stage and smiled faintly. 'He doesn't care for schoolteaching.'

'You seem well acquainted with him.'

'I only did what you wrote me to do,' she answered. 'After I got your letter, I learned a little about him. And I saw that we took the same stage —as you ordered me.'

'All right,' he said. 'What did you find?'

'He's too strong a man to push around,' she said. 'There were some who tried it, and some who tried to buy him. He's a dangerous man when he's angry.'

'He'll join me or leave,' he said harshly. 'I've heard of his reputation. The fighting lawyer! He—' There was a sharp knock on the door and Harkman motioned for her to go into the bedroom.

She shut the door to a fine crack and deliberately leaned against the jamb.

A gravelly voice said, 'I called Wolf and the boys off. But what about the new plan?'

Harkman spoke so softly that she caught only a few words. And they were enough for her to understand what was to take place. Again it was force and the brutal trampling of lesser, weaker men. The hall door slammed and he called to her.

She came out, walking slowly, trying to hide from him her knowledge of his intentions. He was at his desk again, writing. He thrust the pen into a glass of shot and looked up at her.

'I want Lockhart on my side or out of here,' he said. 'And I want to know ahead of time what he plans to do. And what the others plan to do. Those things are your work.'

'I said before—not if you use force again. Not if you kill.'

He came around the desk and loomed over her. 'You'll do as I say!'

She met his gaze. She was not frightened but she lowered her eyes first. 'I'll go now, Clay.'

He took her arm and escorted her to the door. He shut the door quickly to the outside as soon as they were on the stairs, and they made the descent in darkness.

At the ground, he took her hand. 'You'll hear from me,' he said, and drew her toward him, his mouth seeking hers.

She turned her head aside so that his lips touched only her hair. 'This is no place,' she said, and slipped away from him.

His footsteps were quick as he went up the stairs. The door shut and she was alone outside.

*　　*　　*

Joel crossed the street in darkness, slipping between the abandoned buildings opposite the hotel. Behind the buildings, he turned toward the saloon and continued slowly past the row of sagging shacks.

He was abreast of the last one when he heard the opening of the door at the head of the stairs. The brief flash of light revealed Harkman's bulk and then the dark skirts of a woman. He could see no more. The door shut and the sound of light footfalls on the stairs was very clear.

He heard Clay Harkman's voice, 'You'll hear from me.' And then another that took him a moment to recognize, 'This is no place.'

There was the sound of someone mounting the stairs and again the door opened. A thin streak of light flowed down to the ground to touch the dark-haired woman there. It was Juanita Bower and for a moment Joel failed to understand. He waited, motionless, by the corner of the shack.

He caught the faint rustle of her skirt and when she drew even with him he spoke softly, 'Lockhart here.'

She stopped, and now he could see the faint whiteness that was her face. Her voice was low and steady.

'That was a foolish thing to do, Mr. Lockhart. I happen to carry a gun.'

'Your being here is foolish, too,' he said. Moving from the shadow, he stepped closer to her. 'I wasn't spying.'

'But it comes to the same thing, doesn't it,' she said.

'I have no quarrel with you,' Joel said. 'And no desire to hurt you.'

There was silence, both of them standing immobile, each waiting for the other to continue.

He thought of Wolf forcing him back to the hotel, and of Kine going out to guard Lem Happy's safety. Joel had not seen anyone on his second trip across the street, but that did not mean Keno had called off his men or that Kine had stopped patrolling.

'You can't get back without being seen,' he told her.

'I came easily enough.'

'There's been trouble,' he said. 'The hotel is being patrolled.'

She made a soft sound, but he couldn't tell whether of amusement or despair. 'It isn't seemly for a schoolteacher to walk alone at night, is it? And they'll wonder where I've been.'

'As things are,' he answered, 'they'll do more than wonder. They'll ask.'

'I can't tell them,' she said. With a soft rustle of her skirt, she moved away from him. 'But does it matter? You've seen me.'

He spoke impulsively. 'Shall we go? It may be seemly enough if the schoolteacher walks with an escort.'

She stepped closer to him, fumbling in the darkness until she had a hand on his arm. 'Thank you,' she murmured.

The town seemed empty. There was no one in sight. But a moment after they reached the east side of the street a man appeared in the doorway of the hotel, lounging beside it white he cupped a match to his pipe.

'Kine,' Joel said. He glanced at her. 'At least appear as if you were enjoying this.'

She turned her head, finding an instant to laugh at him.

'It was very kind of you, Mr. Lockhart,' she said as they neared Abel Kine. 'Being a stranger and unsettled is a lonesome occupation.'

Joel nodded to Kine as he moved from the doorway to let them pass. 'So I've found,' he said. 'I hope my idea of a walk didn't tire you.'

'Not at all,' she murmured, and smiled without meaning at Kine.

There was no one in the lobby as they passed through. A light came from the kitchen to fall on the stairs but it, too, seemed empty. They went up slowly, pausing before her door. Dipping into the pocket of her dress, she drew out first a small derringer and then a key. Replacing the gun, she handed him the key. When the door was unlocked, he returned it to her.

'Shall I light the lamp for you?'

'If you please.'

The room was like his, but smaller. When the lamp was lighted, he turned up the wick and went back to the door.

She stepped inside, one hand on the latch of the door, and looked him full in the face. Her large dark eyes were questioning and a little frightened, but her expression held the same reserve he had always seen in it.

'Sit down, Mr. Lockhart.' He hesitated but her tone was insistent. She indicated the one chair to him and seated herself on the edge of the bed, her hands folded in her lap.

'Smoke, if you wish.'

'The smell of tobacco—' he began, and stopped.

'No one comes in here,' she said.

He rolled a cigarette slowly and lighted it with equal slowness. Not until then did he look at her again.

'I owe you an explanation.'

He said, 'No explanation is necessary.'

She was smiling faintly. 'Why did you help me?'

'Perhaps,' he said, 'because I've thought for some time that you needed help.'

Her eyebrows raised slightly. 'For some time—since before tonight then?'

'Since the day I first noticed you on the street,' he said. 'And later in the stage.'

'Do you always give your help?'

He made no answer and she stood up, facing him when he rose. Now the full force of her trouble struck him and the words came out of her as if beyond control.

'What is it here? Is it Clay Harkman?'

'Some say it is,' he answered. 'Some here blame him for everything.'

'What is everything?' She saw his hesitation and the reserve left her. 'Please!' She stepped up to him and put her hands on his shoulders, having to reach up only slightly to do so. 'I must know,' she said quickly, sharply. 'Before it goes any further, I must know.'

The strength of her hands surprised him more than the vehemence in her voice.

'You're torturing yourself.'

'Either way it's—' She broke off.

'He wants to make a county quickly,' Joel said. 'Or so they say. And so he's supposed to be bringing in miners and trying to force out the ranchers and farmers. Then, when the time comes, he'll have full control.'

'Do you believe these things?'

'I've seen men do it before,' Joel said. 'It's one way of getting what they want.'

'But if they are true?' she pressed him.

'This isn't my quarrel,' he said to her. 'And nothing has been proved to me. I've fought such things before. I won't do it again until I'm sure.'

'Do you approve of this, then?' She dropped her hands and turned away. When she swung back to him her mouth was curled in scorn. 'Does it mean you'll join him when the time comes to—'

'Did I join such things before?' he struck out at her. Her sudden contempt disturbed him more than had the perfume of her hair.

'I don't really know,' he said, half angry. 'Until I do, all this is just talk. It means nothing.'

'Until you know,' she repeated. She stared at him with a thoughtfulness he could not fathom. He started for the door and she said. 'Let me think—stay, please,' and walked to the window. He reached the door but did not open it.

She swung around and came over to him.

'You don't know,' she said rapidly. 'But I do.' She lifted her head. 'You know of the plan to have Abe Cobble get Cardon to town?' she asked.

'It seems everyone knows of it.'

'It's been changed,' she said quickly. 'I heard Clay give the order. Cobble is to be killed on Cardon's land and Cardon will get the blame.' She took a sharp breath. 'And someone named Gotch is to be made marshal.'

'Why tell me?' he said, half believing.

'So you'll help. So you'll stop him.' She grasped his arm fiercely. 'Clay is afraid of you—you're the one man here he does fear.'

'Why me?'

'For what you were before you came. Don't you think he knows what you did?' Her voice poured out, covering him. 'If you don't join him, he'll try to run you out. Do you think those attacks Markle made on you were by accident? He's afraid you'll lead other men against him—and what he stands for.'

Joel took her hand gently from his arm and held it a moment in his own. 'Just why should this concern you? What is he—was he to you?'

She lifted her face, her eyes wide. The intensity was draining from her, leaving lines of weariness in its place.

'For ten years I've watched him and helped him. I swore every time would be the last. I swore that this time I would not help if it meant killing and crushing others to get what he wanted.'

Despite her words, she was passive. Her hand in his was quiet. 'Who are you that you hate him so?' he asked wonderingly.

'I'm his wife,' she said simply.

'If that is true—'

She sat down on the bed again. 'It's true,' she said wearily. 'There's goodness and strength in you,' she added softly. 'I felt it before—and I felt it more strongly than ever on the stage. Tonight I was sure of it.'

He chose his words carefully. 'What you've just told me has made me your husband's enemy,' he said.

'Some people might say I shot him in the back' she answered.

'That was your choice,' Joel told her. 'You chose to help them—and not him. That was a brave thing.'

'I'm not brave. I'm frightened. If Clay learns—' She drew a deep breath, shivering slightly. 'But I won't ask more of you than of myself.' She smoothered at her dress without watching her hands. 'I was going to run away from it. But not now.'

Joel nodded with understanding. He walked to the door, and she rose, reaching it as he did. He put his hand on the latch and she covered it with her own to detain him a moment.

'Clay won't stop this time,' she said. 'It's his last chance. He's failed too many times before. I saw it in him tonight. Nothing will stop him.'

'Why would a man like Harkman fail?'

'It's his anger,' she said. She saw his surprise and nodded, the faintest of smiles on her lips. 'I know. He's a cold man. He makes plans, one after the other, carefully. He controls himself well—he knows his anger is his weakness. But when he has to plan without careful thought he makes mistakes. Fatal mistakes.'

'It's a good thing to know about an enemy.'

'It's a rotten thing to tell you this—about him!' she cried.

'Do you still love him?'

She looked surprised. 'No—no longer. It died a long time ago. But I wouldn't admit it until tonight. But that gives me no right—I'll say no more against him than I already have. At least leave me that.'

He looked down into her face, into her eyes, and saw the desire for his understanding on her lips. He said, 'I—'

She said, 'Yes?' softly.

He bent his head and her warm mouth came up to meet his, her arms slipping behind his back and holding him to her.

When she withdrew, she murmured, 'I've been afraid of this—for some time.'

'I could take you away,' he said impulsively.

She smiled and there was a sweetness in her he had not suspected before. 'Would we be satisfied—knowing what we left unfinished?'

'No,' he said quietly.

'I'm not free of him,' she agreed. 'Go now. Go quickly.' She drew open the door for him and he stepped into the hall.

In his own room he made no effort to undress but sat before the end window, the room in darkness, the memory of her warm mouth still on his lips.

Staring into the darkness, he realized how deeply he had committed himself. His mouth quirked in a bitter smile. What the logical pleading of his friends could not do, a few words from a woman had done.

He rose restlessly, remembering that he had not yet seen Keno or Cobble.

He checked his gun and found his heavy coat, then stepped to the doorway and went softly along the darkened hall. He slowed involuntarily by her door. As if by a signal, it opened.

Lamplight from within flowed around her. She wore a loose wrapper over her white nightdress and her feet were bare beneath it. The long, black shimmer of her hair cascaded down her back, giving her a youthful appearance despite the weariness still on her face. She held a hairbrush in one hand. She stood completely natural, knowing he would understand.

Her eyes touched his gun and then his impassive face. ‘Be careful—Joel.’

‘I won’t fight your husband unless I have to,’ he said slowly. ‘But if something should happen to him—then I’ll come for you.’

She stepped into the hall, her feet soundless on the carpetless boards. ‘Don’t pledge yourself.’

He lifted a hand, brushing at the heavy sweep of hair just above her forehead. ‘I do pledge myself,’ he said. ‘A man can’t deny what’s inside him.’

‘Nor a woman,’ she said. ‘But Clay is still my husband.’

He dropped his hand. 'The pledge stands.'

She stepped back inside the room. '*Vaya condios,*' she said in Spanish. 'Go with God.'

The door closed, shutting her away from him. He went on down the stairs, still slowly and softly.

'Lockhart!'

He lifted his head. It was Jed Hopper, standing in the kitchen doorway, his grizzled features wary as he watched Joel descend the stairway. There no longer seemed to be any trace of friendliness about him. 'Going hunting at midnight?'

At the foot of the stairs, Joel stopped. 'Hunting trouble,' he said. 'It's like getting a cougar—do it before he kills your cattle.'

'All quiet now,' Jed said. 'They quit wasting time on Lem.'

'I saw Kine out front a while ago,' Joel remarked.

The wariness still held in Jed Hopper's usually goodnatured glance. 'Sleeping,' he said, pointing to the lobby settee.

'If Cobble is,' Joel answered, 'I'll wake him out of it.'

'Cobble or Harkman?' The old man's voice was flat with suspicion.

'Meaning what?' Joel asked.

'If Lem don't see it, it ain't seen,' Jed Hopper said. 'And I figure anyone so interested in Harkman's woman would be interested in him, too.'

Joel relaxed. This was something he could understand. 'I am interested in Harkman,' he said equably. 'I'm going to try and stop him.'

Skepticism darkened Jed Hopper's face. 'Mighty sudden,' he said dryly.

Anger at the man's foolishness struggled up in Joel. 'My business,' he answered, and started for the door.

'I wouldn't, Lockhart!'

The bull-whip snap of Hopper's voice spun Joel around. He had been joined by Lem Happy, who stood easily, his old rifle in the crook of his arm.

'You think—?'

'I think,' Hopper interrupted in a flat tone, 'that you'd do best to stay like you was. Out of the way. This ain't nothing we can't handle.'

Joel saw their plan to circumvent Harkman was made and they were afraid he would wreck it. The humor of the situation struck him, but it was empty amusement. He shook his head at the two men and continued on across the lobby.

Abel Kine's mild voice came from the dimness by the settee. 'I think Hopper's a mite mixed, Lockhart, but for now I'm backing him up.'

'It looks,' Joel said dryly, 'as if I don't go for my walk.' He returned to the stairs and started up them, stopping to glance down at Jed Hopper. 'You called this one,' he said. 'But you'd do better to listen to Kine than to your own thoughts.'

He slept easily, wakening with the first faint light from the east. He washed in cold water and then went to the side window to study the yard below. The cedar-shake roof of a lean-to woodshed was against the hotel, directly beneath him. Beyond that stood the small horse barn backed up against the steep hillside. Only bare ground lay in between. He could see no sign of life, no movement.

Getting his gun belt and heavy coat, he opened the window slowly. It was a small opening, so that he had to twist his shoulders after he had thrust his feet and body through. Letting loose his grip, he lit with his knees bent and his hands reaching for the rough log walls of the building to steady himself. He held the position a moment. But there was no sound beyond the restless stamping of an animal in the barn, and he eased himself quietly to the yard.

The animal warmth of the barn struck him as he stepped in and for a moment he stood still, unable to see. When his eyes adjusted to the gloom, he could make out three horses and a mule, a rack of saddle and bridles. He slipped one of the bridles on the nearest horse. Then he spent a moment holding his hand close to the animal's nostril's, stroking him so that he might understand that here was a friend and not be disturbed.

The horse allowed himself to be saddled

and led into the yard. Joel mounted and reined toward the far side of the hotel, going around it to the road. When he was let out, the bay made a few stiff-legged hops of pleasure and then cut loose up the wagon road toward its meeting with the river.

When they started into Whispering Canyon the sky narrowed above to a thin gray slice so that there was little light. As they climbed, the wind made itself felt, and Joel could hear its soft sibilance over the river noises below. At the top of the pass, Joel slipped off his heavy coat and tied it behind the saddle.

In the valley the wind was stilled and it was very quiet.

Joel touched his heels to the horse, bitter in his thoughts at what might lie ahead. He was nearly to the shoulder of hillside that sheltered the 2C ranch when the horse stopped, stiff-legged and half rearing back.

Joel glanced up and saw another horse, saddled, grazing just across a thicket of leafless Juneberry and wild rose. He followed the line of the thicket with his eyes, past the point where his horse had stopped. A pair of booted feet were thrust into the trail.

'Easy,' Joel said. He patted the bay's neck and climbed down. Holding the reins, he advanced cautiously. But the feet and legs of the man were quiet, and when he parted the tangle of bushes and peered in he saw only what he had expected.

CHAPTER EIGHT

Lace curtain was stirring when Joel drove Tim Cardon's wagon slowly along the street. Gil Abbey rode beside Joel and the bay horse and Abbey's pinto walked the length of their lead ropes behind. In the wagon box Abe Cobble lay under canvas.

Joel pulled the team up before the hotel. Abel Kine lounged in the doorway as he had the night before, his stubby pipe clenched between his teeth. He shook his head at sight of Joel but came forward to the edge of the board sidewalk.

'Lem Happy don't appreciate having his horse rid by strangers.'

Kine went to the rear of the wagon and untied the bay from the lead rope. He studied the lumpy canvas in the box and then raised his bearded face to Joel.

'Get what you went for?'

'Found him so,' Joel said. 'It's Cobble.'

'As I thought,' Kine said. He waited, his heavy hands holding the horse's reins loosely, his faraway eyes still on Joel. 'Taking him to Harkman?' he asked finally.

'Where else?'

Kine nodded, 'Coming back?'

'I'll get back,' Joel said. He looped the reins over the whipstock and took out his tobacco.

'He was in the brush on the 2C trail. Not a half mile from Tim's.'

'I thought that, too,' Kine said. 'Where's Cardon?'

'Home,' Joel told him.

Abbey made a torn, laughing sound. 'About hogtied,' he said.

Joel passed his tobacco to Abbey and then licked and lit his cigarette. He smoked thoughtfully.

'Tell Happy thanks for the horse,' he said to Kine. Picking up the reins, he clucked the team into motion. As they passed the general store, he saw Nora Reeves on the steps with a broom and he lifted his hat to her. She nodded without pleasantness until she saw Abbey and then broke into a quick smile, lifting her broom in a wave. Across the street and up a way, a swamper was cleaning the saloon, also with a broom. Joel drew the wagon to the sidewalk and leaned toward him.

'Call Harkman down for me.'

The swamper spat and shook his head. 'He don't call. Go get them.'

Joel said, 'Team and all?' and started the horses, over the walk and up toward the front step. The swamper took one startled look and broke from the door. Joel reined the team to a stop with the wheels against the edge of the sidewalk.

'This isn't smart,' Abbey warned him.

'No reason for you to get mixed up in it,'

Joel said. 'Go visit with Miss Nora.'

Abbey looked over his shoulder and then at the front of the saloon. 'I'll stay,' he said reluctantly.

Keno pushed the saloon doors open. He had to step around the team to come near the wagon.

'What's this, Lockhart?'

'I want to see Harkman,' Joel said pleasantly. 'I've got something for him.'

'I'll take it.' Keno stopped a few feet away, flicking his cold eyes from the two men to the wagon box. 'What's that?'

'Don't you know?'

Keno studied him coldly. 'Why should I know?'

'Go get Harkman,' Joel said.

Keno reached the side of the wagon box with two long strides and jerked back the canvas. He let it fall almost immediately and swung about, slapping his gun from his hip with the movement.

Joel laughed. His own gun was in his lap, his hand smoothly around the butt. 'Not yet,' he said.

They held it that way, neither man moving. Keno's eyes held the glitter of anger. Abbey made a motion with his hand and Keno's gun flicked in his direction, settling him into quiet.

'Keep out of it,' Joel said quietly.

Clay Harkman broke it up, stepping from the saloon and around the horses. 'What is it,

Keno?' He looked at Joel, no expression on his face. 'So?'

'Brought Cobble back to you,' Joel said. 'He was getting stiff when I found him. He's yours.' He continued to watch Keno, though he talked to Harkman.

'What's your interest?' Harkman demanded.

'I was riding,' Joel said, 'and I found him.'

'You ride to Cardon's early,' Keno said sharply.

Joel's smile was a quick thinning of his lips. 'Cardon's? Did I say Cardon's? You know a lot about it, Keno.'

Keno's mouth moved silently and he took his eyes off Joel long enough to glance at Harkman. 'It's Cardon's team and wagon,' he said.

Joel shook his head. 'Do you pick your men for their brains, Harkman?'

The team, growing restless, stepped about, and Harkman moved back. He looked at Joel and nodded, understanding coming to him now. His expression did not change.

'You're not playing this smart.'

'My way,' Joel said shortly. He had counted on more reaction than this.

'Your way,' Harkman repeated. 'I've been waiting to learn that.' Their eyes met, Joel no longer bothering with Keno. He could see the man's mind working, seeking a way to shape a new plan quickly.

'I won't wait all day. He was your man—

take him,' Joel said.

Harkman went to the wagon and lifted the canvas. Keno stood, his gun still ready. Harkman looked coldly at him. 'Go get some men for this.'

Keno thrust his gun into his holster and left them.

Joel looked behind Harkman at the street. Hopper was coming slowly from the hotel, limping along the board sidewalk. Elmira Reeves stood on the steps of her store and she held a rifle by its barrel, the butt resting near her foot. A steady hammering from the blacksmith shop rang out. Sam Teel was working away at his fence straddling.

Harkman reached down and unpinned the star from Cobble's chest. 'He won't need this,' he said. 'The new marshal can wear it to find his killer.' He glanced up at Joel, holding the star in his hand, his lips smiling. 'Any suggestions, Lockhart?'

Joel thought, *Here is his plan.* But Harkman had made it too quickly, and it was easy to see the weaknesses in it. 'Take a vote. Now.'

Harkman shook his head, still smiling. Keno came out at that moment with Leppy Gotch and the long-trunked man called Wolf. Leppy reached into the wagon and lifted Cobble, canvas and all. He shifted the feet to Wolf and, silently, they went into the saloon.

'Send the word,' Harkman said to Keno. 'Lockhart wants an election.'

‘Not that way,’ Joel said quietly. ‘We’ll call it now or make a list of eligible voters.’

‘Meaning what?’ Harkman asked.

‘No transient miners. No drifters.’

‘Five farmers, two ranchers, and that side of town,’ Harkman said. ‘You want it too easy, Lockhart.’ He made a pushing motion with his hand. ‘Keno, get Leppy back out here.’

Joel remained quiet, knowing that he had Harkman on edge now. He saw Jed Hopper reach Elmira Reeves and come with her down the sidewalk toward the wagon. Beside him, Gil Abbey still sat quietly. Sam Teel’s hammer rang out louder than before.

Leppy Gotch came to the steps, blinking and looking inquiringly at Harkman. Harkman motioned to him and, when he stepped around the team, reached up and pinned the star to his chest.

‘No,’ Joel said.

‘Yes,’ Harkman answered. ‘He was Cobble’s deputy—didn’t you know? He’ll take over until we get this election business straight.’

Keno, on the steps, gave Joel a thin smile. Joel stood up, looking toward Elmira Reeves and Jed Hopper, now in the center of the street. Elmira Reeves shifted the weight of her rifle and stared at him.

‘What do you say?’ he called to her.

‘Leppy Gotch won’t be marshal on our side of town!’ she retorted angrily.

‘This is foolishness,’ Harkman said. ‘Just

until a proper election—'

'Until a proper election,' Joel said dryly, 'I suggest we make Jed Hopper marshal.'

Elmira nodded vigorously. Joel saw Harkman's mouth draw out fine. Leppy Gotch seemed unaware of what was taking place. He was looking down at his star with a thick, surprised smile.

'As Cobble's deputy,' Harkman said, 'Leppy—'

Joel said, 'Let Leppy Gotch tend bar where he belongs. You had your way about the first marshal, Harkman.'

Elmira Reeves made a move to step forward and Jed Hopper put a restraining hand on her arm. She shook it off. Harkman stared over the wagon box at her. 'I say Gotch!'

'Not on my side of the street,' she answered him.

Abbey stirred and Joel put out a hand, quieting him. He said, 'Let Gotch be marshal in your saloon, Harkman. Jed Hopper can take the rest of the town. Until election,' he added mockingly.

'Have it that way then!' Harkman cried. He walked around the wagon to the center of the street, stopping just short of Elmira Reeves. With his boot toe he made a rough mark in the half-frozen dirt.

'Gotch is marshal west of this line.' He swung around. Fury had drawn his face white, and his mouth twisted beneath the line of his mustache. 'Hold Lockhart, Leppy. He's our witness to Cobble's killing.'

Leppy Gotch blinked at Harkman and then, with surprising quickness, made a grab for the bridle of the near horse with his huge hand.

Joel backed the team and swung forward as the front wheels cleared the edge of the sidewalk. Leppy Gotch closed his hand over the bridle. Joel reached for the whip, lifting it and bringing it across Leppy's neck. He winced and drew back. Joel flicked the whip over the horses' rumps and they leaped forward, careening the wagon and bolting down the road.

He pulled them around just beyond the jailhouse and came down the east side of the street. Jed Hopper and Elmira were standing in the same place but now Elmira's rifle was lifted. He heard her say, 'You'll shoot no one, Keno.'

Keno's gun went slowly back into its holster and the cold quiet of strained silence settled down. Joel stopped the team.

Harkman's voice rang out, under control again. 'You're a wanted man in my town, Lockhart!'

* * *

In his office, Harkman spent an hour bent over his desk, his pen whipping sharply over a sheet of paper. Finally the remains of his anger dulled and he lighted a cigar, settling back to think.

Then he rose and went to the door, calling down. When Keno came to the foot of the stairs, Harkman said, 'Get Markle and Leppy in here.' He went back to his desk and waited, his cigar idle between his fingers. He made no move until they had filed into the room.

'You bungled,' he said to Keno.

Keno turned his narrow eyes on Markle. 'He did,' he said.

Markle rubbed his shaking hand over his face. 'You got what you wanted, didn't you?'

Harkman shut him off with a savage gesture. 'Why didn't someone stop Lockhart? You were supposed to find Cobble yourself and bring him in with Cardon. What made you think you had all day to get back out there?'

Getting up, he took short, quick steps around the room. 'You, Keno—you were supposed to get Cardon in here to answer to a charge of murder. Now we have nothing to bargain with.' He stopped and sat down. They were only what he had created—all three of them—and cursing them would solve nothing.

'I heard Hopper had Lockhart shut in,' Keno said. 'And I didn't figure Lockhart was working for them, nohow.'

'He is now.' Harkman took the stub of his cigar and shredded it between his fingers. He looked at Markle. 'You didn't want to wait to go to work on Lockhart. All right, you're through waiting—if you think you can handle him.'

Markle rubbed the butt of his gun, thinking of the way he had been roughed up, both in the saloon and outside. 'I can handle him.' He grinned meaningly at Leppy Gotch. The big man had been standing in silence. Now he lifted his head as Harkman spoke his name sharply.

'If Hopper or Lockhart comes across the middle of the street, get them.'

Leppy's huge head bobbed. 'Put them in jail?' he asked mildly.

Seth Markle spewed out laughter. 'What jail? Cobble's old shack that—' Harkman's expression stopped his laughter, drying it within him.

'Out of the mouths of fools,' Harkman murmured. He looked thoughtfully at Leppy. 'All right, we'll get the jailhouse—tonight. We'll get two teams and skid it over to this side.' He saw Keno about to speak and waved him to silence.

One thing he became sure of—taking the jailhouse should be their first blow. The other side had it now. When he had it he would hold the symbol of law and order.

'Tonight,' he repeated.

'It'll mean a fight,' Keno said.

'Then,' Harkman said, 'make sure there are enough men in town.

*   *   *

Jed Hopper took a lamp from the hotel desk and handed it to Elmira Reeves. 'It's a woman's job,' he said. 'It ain't something I could handle.'

'It isn't anything I want to handle,' she said tartly. 'I scarcely know the woman. And just because Harkman was mixed up in getting her here doesn't mean anything. She may be as respectable as you or I.'

'Or more so,' Hopper said with a flash of his old humor. 'But that ain't it, Elmira. He was too danged insistent that she be the schoolteacher. Maybe that don't mean much, either, but Lem Happy saw her at his place last night. She went in and stayed a spell and when she came out Lockhart was waiting for her.'

'Then let Joel answer for her.'

'I ain't too sure about Lockhart,' Hopper said.

'After today?' She snorted. 'Jed Hopper, you're a fool. An old fool!'

'Lockhart got Harkman what he wanted, the way I see it. The whole thing's broke open now—and we wasn't ready. Harkman can get a dozen men to our one.' He touched her shoulder. 'You just go up and find out how that woman stands. We don't want none of Harkman's help on this side now. We can't afford it, Elmira.'

She sighed, and then started up the stairs.

Elmira Reeves was a firm, outspoken woman, seldom awed by anything, but when she rapped on the door and had been asked in, she found this steady, dark-eyed person somehow disconcerting. Juanita offered her the chair and took a seat on the bed herself. She did not seem surprised at the visit.

'I've been expecting you, Mrs. Reeves,' she said cordially. 'I want to get the school organized as soon as possible. Even if we wait until fall to open, it will take some time to get ready.'

The very attitude of innocence she would normally accept now angered Elmira. That and the woman's quiet sureness. 'You don't hear much, do you?' she burst out. She tried to catch herself. It was not at all the way she had planned to start this. But she had gone too far and so she kept on, 'Clay Harkman has split the town.'

Juanita kept her eyes fixed on the older woman's face.

'Is that my concern?' she asked.

'If you belong across the street,' Elmira said, 'now is the time to go.'

'I—belong there?'

'You were seen with Clay Harkman last night, and with Joel Lockhart afterward!'

Juanita smiled. If was a genuine, warm smile of relief. She could think now, and a dozen simple defenses presented themselves. But she hesitated.

There was only one thing for her to do—go to Clay and try to stop him from continuing this. If he wouldn't, then she would tell him she was leaving. Meanwhile, it wouldn't be fair for her to stay here in the other camp.

She rose, bowing her head. 'If what you think is so,' she said, 'then I have no further right here.'

'I don't know what it means,' Elmira Reeves confessed. 'We can't have spies here.'

Juanita's head came up, her eyes flashing. 'Get out, Mrs. Reeves. I'll go, but I'm doing so of my own choice. Not driven by your suspicions.'

Elmira backed hastily toward the door. Then she realized her situation and drew herself up.

'Your bags will be sent,' she said coldly, and went out.

Juanita stood motionless, letting her temper drain out. At first she was angry with Elmira. But soon she began to wonder if she might not have done the same if the circumstances had been reversed. It was Clay, she knew. Wherever he was, tensions grew—whatever he touched became soiled.

She stirred and started to pack, wondering how Joel would judge her from this.

She passed through the dim lobby, stepping into the cool dark of the night without seeing anyone. The man Joel had called Kine came from the darkness beyond the hotel door. He was smoking his pipe and he looked at her incuriously, nodding but not offering to speak.

There were a number of horses coming into town and after they had passed, she crossed the street. She turned at the far side and went toward the saloon, walking very slowly.

At the saloon corner, she turned and went alongside the building to the rear stairway. There were a number of horses hitched at the back. They showed clearly when someone opened the door to go in, letting light out into the yard. She paid little attention beyond a dull curiosity and climbed the stairs. She tried the door and found it open. Remembering from last night, she walked along the hall to the front, and knocked on the door.

Clay Harkman came after a moment, opening it and staring out at her. 'What are you doing here?'

Suddenly she found it amusing, and she laughed.

'I was sent,' she said. With deliberate coquetry, she put out her hands. 'Where else does Clay Harkman's wife belong but on his side of the line?'

CHAPTER NINE

From noon, men rode in—men Joel had never seen before, more than he had known existed in these parts. All of them swung to the rear of the saloon, and none rode out again. Only one of the farmers came to town that day and when he saw what was taking place at Harkman's he hurried home.

'Harkman's gathering an army,' Joel said.

'See it,' Hopper said. 'When dark comes I'll send Lem over to find out what's up.' He shook his head. 'We ain't got the strength, no matter what it is they're planning. We got a dozen, he'll get fifty.'

'And five hundred if he chooses to let out the news about the gold strike on Gil's creek,' Elmira said.

'It's his ace,' Joel told them. 'He won't play it until there's no other way. Fifty miners he can control. Five hundred might decide to control him.'

'You got any more ideas?' Hopper demanded sourly. His voice was riled and Joel realized he objected to what had been done that morning. It had come too fast for him.

Joel said, 'Harkman's a planner, and it's good tactics to hit a planner before his plans are set. Hit him so he has to make changes and hit him again before he can get set. Keep him off balance.'

'Start hitting then,' Hopper said.

'Did that farmer take the word back with him?'

'I sent Happy out for that job,' Hopper said.

Joel looked up the street, noticing the long

shadows stretching from the west. 'I'll take the team back,' he said, 'and try to keep Tim and Abbey at home.'

'We'll need all the men we can get here,' Hopper objected.

'They can block Whispering Canyon against an army—and we might all need to hole up there if things don't work out.'

Hopper spat out through the door and shut it tightly. 'Do it your way,' he said.

As he went to the team and wagon, Joel passed Nora Reeves coming from her house. Her nod was more friendly than it had been during the morning. 'Tell Gil to be careful,' she said.

'I'll say the same to you,' he answered. 'Abbey can handle himself.'

'And so can I,' she said. She stopped by the wagon and stroked the neck of the off horse. 'I'm glad you did that this morning.'

'Jed Hopper isn't.'

'He's stubborn,' she said, 'But he'll see. And when he does, he'll be big enough to admit it.' She turned and went on a few paces and looked back, offering him a friendly smile. 'Don't forget to tell Gil to be careful.'

He touched his hat to her and took up the reins. He drove carefully, the rifle he had borrowed on the floor at his feet.

He thought of Juanita and his anger rose against Clay Harkman. She had told Joel what she knew. Not to hurt her husband but to protect the town. Doing so had torn her, he could see that. And his admiration grew with his understanding of the conflict she must have faced within herself.

When he swung into Cordon's yard the sun had sunk and it was already half dark. Abbey was there, by the horse trough with Tim, and Abbey offered to take the team to the barn when Joel climbed down. Tim's face was squeezed as he looked inquiringly at Joel.

'Harkman's getting an army in.'

'Told you this would bust wide open,' Tim said. He twisted to Abbey as he came back from the barn. 'Let's ride.'

'No,' Joel said. 'Both of you stay here.' He shook his head at Tim's angry movement. 'Don't throw all your force in at once. Harkman has too many. Our time's coming.'

'A fight's a fight,' Tim said impatiently. 'I'm tired of waiting.'

'Lockhart's right,' Abbey said. 'Harkman's too strong right now.'

'Tim,' Joel said, 'can you put up the town women? If it gets too bad, we'll move them out.

'I can,' Abbey said quickly.

'Either way,' Joel told him, and he thought of how eager Abbey sounded at the chance to have Nora Reeves near by.

Tim spat his cigarette to the ground and put his boot toe on the spark. 'Ask Ellen. I won't be here—I'll be in town.'

Joel gave a sour grin, nodded to Abbey, and went on into the house. Ellen was washing her supper dishes but she stopped long enough to bring Joel a plate of food and pour him a cup of coffee.

'Don't just sit there!' she said sharply. 'What's going on?'

He told her briefly. 'See that Tim stays. There'll be no fighting yet unless someone gets touchy and starts shooting.'

'That would be Tim,' she admitted. She pushed a lock of dark hair from her face and slumped wearily at the table. 'What'll they do now with the new schoolteacher?'

Joel blew on his coffee softly, his eyes meeting hers over the top of the cup. 'Her concern is teaching, not fighting.'

'Abbey brought the news. Lem Happy told Jed he saw her leaving Harkman's last night.'

He made no comment but began to eat. His sister spoke again, obviously irritated with him.

'If that's true, she'll have to go.'

'You all judge too soon,' Joel said. 'She's a fine woman. She deserves none of this.'

'No woman of Clay Harkman's could be fine.'

'Your hatred is making you foolish,' he said.

'I see,' she said quietly. 'I heard, too, that you met her last night.'

'I say again, you judge too soon. If anyone trusts me—you should be the one.' He returned to his eating. When Tim came inside he was ready to leave.

'Abbey rode home,' Tim said. 'This is worrying him.'

'It should,' Joel agreed. He looked at Tim steadily. 'In town this morning he used his head. He kept it in a tight situation.' He twisted a cigarette into shape and bent to the lamp, sucking a light up the chimney. 'Now lend me a horse, Tim.'

'I'm ready,' Tim said.

'We may need this valley. Someone has to stay and defend it.' Tim shook his head stubbornly and Joel added, 'Your time will come.'

'Time? When is the time? I've lost so much beef I don't dare butcher one for meat. How much longer do I wait?'

'Not long,' Joel said. 'Perhaps not long enough.' He paused and smiled briefly at his sister to show her their quarrel had no more meaning. 'Do I get that horse, Tim?'

It was a good mount, a sturdy, close-coupled black gelding, and Joel made fast time. In the distance he could see the lights of Lace Curtain, a stronger glow against the clouds than he thought they could make. Arriving, he saw the reason. The store and the blacksmith shop were lighted, as well as the saloon and the hotel. From the saloon came the sound of many men.

He swung behind the hotel and turned the horse into the small barn. He left the saddle, snapping the black up short to the manger so he couldn't roll. The horse nickered in protest and Joel slapped his rump.

'This is no time to undress,' he said, and hurried out.

He went into the hotel through the kitchen, carrying the rifle he had taken from the wagon. He found Nora Reeves behind the hotel desk, and he saw that she had a rifle as well. It lay across the desk top, leveled at him. When he stepped into the lamplight, she relaxed, trying to laugh a little.

'They're going to take the jailhouse. Jed is down there now.'

He nodded to her and started back out. 'Abbey is staying home,' he said. 'He'll be safe enough.'

'I'm glad,' was all she said, but her smile of thanks told more than words.

He went out, going behind buildings to the jailhouse. As he reached the door a man detached himself from shadow.

'Lockhart here,' Joel said softly.

'You heard then?' It was Abel Kine's voice.

'I heard,' Joel said. He opened the door and stepped in, calling out his name again.

'Up front,' Jed Hopper grunted from the darkness. He still sounded sour and when Joel had groped his way forward, he said, 'We ain't ready for this.'

'I'm ready,' Joel said. 'Harkman will have it figured for a surprise. So maybe he won't fight for it.'

'What's he got all them miners in town for—to have a birthday party?'

Joel let it go. The saloon across the way was so brightly lighted that some of its glow came into the jailhouse, outlining the desk and chair that comprised the furniture. It showed Hopper as a thick lump, but the light was not strong enough for Joel to make out his features.

'The farmers?' Joel asked Hopper.

'Around,' Hopper said. 'We sent Teel home and put men in the cupola of his shop. And we got a couple upstairs in the hotel. One's in the store with Elmira. Happy's over there, again.'

'Someday he's going to get caught,' Joel said.

Hopper spat on the floor and chuckled a little proudly. 'You don't shoot what you don't see or hear. Or what moves too fast to aim at.' He paused and spat again. 'The schoolteacher went over to Harkman's.'

Joel was glad when a sudden dimming of the saloon lights kept him from the necessity of a reply.

The lights were going out one by one in the saloon, and finally there was only a faint glow left, leaving the street and jailhouse in heavy darkness.

'It's coming,' Joel said.

For long minutes they stood watching but seeing nothing. The noises from the saloon were muted but at last came the clanking of harness chains.

'Teams,' Hopper said. 'They're figuring on snaking it over there.'

Joel could barely make them out now. Two six-horse teams, and by the sound they were dragging heavy log chains. The teams came slowly around the saloon and headed for the center of the street.

'No shooting if we can help it,' Joel said warningly. He took the time to roll a cigarette and then he struck a match, letting the flame light his face at the window before he bent to fire the cigarette.

'Hold those teams!' he called out.

There was no change in their steady pace, nor any answer from across the way.

'Lay a warning shot in front,' Joel suggested.

Hopper fired his rifle. Mud spurted in front of the nearer team and the lead horses reared in sudden terror. They twisted their harness as they went up and the animals behind them were thrown to one side and down, neighing shrilly as they floundered, throwing the whole team awry. A man from behind them swore violently as he worked the lines.

'No closer,' Joel called. 'Hear me, Harkman?'

Harkman's voice was clear above the sounds of the threshing team. 'If you want shooting, we'll give it to you!'

'We want nothing but peace,' Joel said. He

could make out Harkman against the front wall of the saloon now.

'This is our jail, Lockhart. Cobble had it built. Cobble's man will use it.'

'It stays on this side of the line,' Joel answered.

'We're coming after it.'

'You'll lose your horses,' Joel said flatly. 'Save your lead, Harkman, and maybe Hopper will sell you the jail tomorrow.'

From behind him Jed Hopper laughed. A gun went off. Splinter chipped from the side of the window frame beside Joel. Hopper threw up his rifle and shot for the door, getting a cry of pain in return.

'Stop it!' Harkman cried. 'No more of that, you fools. Not until I give the word. Keno, keep them in line.'

There was another silence, both sides waiting. The team still on its feet had stopped and the other was being unharnessed by two men moving about in the dark.

'They ain't through,' Hopper whispered.

'Lost his surprise,' Joel said. 'He needs a new attack. He'll kill, but not until he has to.'

Suddenly Harkman shouted an order, sending the teams back. 'All right, Lockhart,' he called out. 'For now!'

'For now,' Joel mocked him. 'But we stay, Jed,' he said in a lower tone.

The saloon doors swung open again as men went inside and the teams were led away.

Joel watched, waiting for a trick. A sound from the rear spun him around, but a sharp, breathless giggle caused him to relax. It was Lem Happy.

'They're sending a crew for Cardon,' he said. 'They say they're going to lock him in *their* jailhouse.'

'They ain't got a jailhouse,' Jed Hopper said grimly.

'Maybe they expect us to ride to Cardon's,' Joel said. 'Maybe they let Happy overhear them.'

'I was quiet,' Happy said in an aggrieved tone. 'And Harkman had Gotch deputize Markle and a crew. They're ready to ride.'

'They won't get through the pass,' Joel said.

'A man just came in,' Happy said. 'Tim and Abbey ain't at the pass.'

Joel said quietly, 'Can you hold it, Hopper?'

'I held jails before,' Jed Hopper said.

Joel went out as he had come, getting his horse from the barn behind the hotel. He mounted and rode cautiously to the corner of the hotel. The road was empty, but he could make out the faint sounds of a single horseman to the north. He listened briefly, and decided the rider was going away from town. Likely one of Harkman's crew, he thought, and spurred onto the road.

His hope had been to get to Tim and Abbey and have them at the pass before Markle and his men got there, but now he could only hope to overtake the rider ahead and find the meaning of it. He dug in his heels again, pushing the horse faster.

'Joel!'

He turned in the saddle, not sure of the voice, unable to separate the sound from the pounding hooves of his mount. He could see nothing behind him. Again he thought he caught the voice, but he could not be sure.

'No time, anyway,' he said, and spurred on.

CHAPTER TEN

Juanita waited openly in Harkman's office. Men drifted in and out, most of them removing their hats and staring when they saw her but none speaking except to Harkman.

She heard them formulate the plan to take the jail, smoothing out the details under Harkman's direction, and finally she had to rise and go into the bedroom.

She went to the window and looked down at the street. Face pressed against the glass, she waited. She heard the shot that Jed Hopper laid across the horses and the shot aimed at Joel and the answer Jed Hopper gave, drawing a cry from someone below her. She heard the exchange between Joel and Clay and she felt a momentary relief.

When she heard men coming into the office,

she moved from the window to stand by the door. She was in time to hear a man swear viciously. It was Keno's rumbling voice.

'Then,' Harkman said, 'he heard we're sending a crew out to get Cardon?'

There was a brief silence and then Harkman said, 'Good. It worked out then.'

Keno made a grunting sound of inquiry. Harkman went on, 'I just sent Markle out to the pass. There'll be no crew going to Cardon's until Markle gets back.'

Keno said something too low for Juanita to catch. Harkman's answer was louder. 'First we get Lockhart and then the jailhouse and then Cardon to put in it.' His voice rose. 'I'll waste no more time.'

'What do we do until Markle brings him back—if he does?'

'He will,' Harkman answered. 'As soon as Lockhart rides out, put a ring around the jailhouse.'

Juanita felt her knees buckle under the impact of Clay's words. She held to the frame of the door, holding herself upright with the strength of her grip. He would not stop for her now. He had his plan and he would break on it before he would stop.

They were gone. She opened the door and went into the office, then to the desk. She rummaged through it until she found what she sought. It was a Colt .44.

Her mouth was an ugly line of

determination as she stepped into the hall, the gun held before her. She reached the rear door and slipped through without challenge. She made a quiet descent to the ground but as she reached it, a man's burly figure rose up against the dark.

'Who's that?'

'Mrs. Harkman,' she said. She was surprised to hear her voice so steady.

'Haw! Mrs. Harkman. Lady, no one goes out tonight.'

She stepped up to him and thrust the gun against his side. 'Turn around and walk ahead of me.'

Her voice held no hint of indecision. The man turned quickly and went ahead of her. She shifted the gun to her left hand, not taking the muzzle from his back, and with her right drew his gun from its holster.

They stayed behind the old buildings until they were opposite the hotel, then she lifted the gun in her right hand and brought it with all her strength against his skull. He made a choking sound and she struck him again. He bent at the knees, falling face forward at her feet.

As she reached the sidewalk, a horse came around the far side of the hotel. In the light from the lobby window she had a brief glimpse of the rider and she stumbled forward into the street.

'Joel!'

She thought he twisted in the saddle but then he was gone, though she shouted his name again. She hurried across the street, and walked into the lobby.

'Stop!'

She drew up to see Nora Reeves at the hotel desk. A rifle lay across its top, leveled at her.

'I want a horse quickly.'

Nora Reeves looked at the gun and at Juanita's disheveled hair. 'I heard you calling,' she said coldly.

Juanita's patience flared and burned out. 'I want a horse!' she cried. 'Markle's at the pass, waiting for him.'

Nora Reeves did not move, nor did her rifle. 'You belong across the street,' she said.

'You fool!' Juanita walked on as if she had not been stopped, hurrying through the kitchen and into the yard.

She found the horse barn and spent a few moments saddling the smaller of the two horses inside. She had him out and was ready to mount when Nora Reeves came from the hotel.

'I'm going to warn him,' Juanita called to her. Nora ran past her, stumbling over the uneven ground as she hurried toward the store.

Juanita grasped the horn, drew herself into the saddle and swung toward the road. She lashed the horse with her rein, feeling him leap under her into the night.

The horse seemed to know the road even in darkness and she had only to ride and not to guide him. The force of his running worked at her hair until it was loose so that it fell and then blew back behind her.

After what seemed an endless time she began to feel the dampness of the river and then its faint wet smell came to her. She could see little in the darkness but there was a canyon wall to her right now and the horse had slowed as if mounting a grade. She guessed that this was the pass, and felt thankful that the horse knew the road.

Suddenly she caught the roar of a gun ahead of her. It was loud, the noise trapped in the canyon walls. In a moment she saw the flicker of a light that grew larger until it became a lantern held in the air. The man holding the lantern was peering at her, and she recognized Seth Markle.

The lantern cast a dull yellowish light over the scene. Markle stood with his gun pointed at her. At his feet, Joel lay stretched on his back. At the edge of the pool of light a single horse was tethered to a small tree. Joel's gun was still in its holster; he had had no chance to draw.

She sat motionless, watching the gun in Markle's hand. He spoke, peering toward her in surprise.

'Who . . . Oh, Harkman's woman.' His eyes continued to study her. 'What are you doing here?'

'Harkman's wife,' she corrected him. And when he lowered his own gun slightly, she raised hers and shot him.

Markle made a hurt sound and went backward, his gun clattering to the rocky floor of the pass and the lantern making an arc of light as he fell. He cursed and righted himself, going for the gun he had dropped. But she was off her horse, standing over Joel and looking at Markle.

'Leave it there,' she said coldly.

Now he swore again. 'My arm,' he whined at her.

'Stay there or it'll be your heart,' she said. She kept the gun in her hand and knelt, running her fingers beneath Joel's coat, keeping her eyes on Markle. She drew out her hand, having felt no blood, and then, placed it over his heart. The feel of it beating strongly through his clothing washed her with relief.

'Where did you hit him?'

'Scraped his head,' he whined. 'He ain't hurt bad.'

'But you tried,' she said softly. 'Bring that light closer,' she ordered. He did not move and she motioned with the gun. He came then and she had him set the lantern near her. She made him back off.

'Bring your horse!'

He walked sullenly to the horse and led him back. She took Joel's gun from his holster and stepped back.

'Tie him to the saddle—carefully.'

'My arm,' Markle said again. But after a moment he went to work.

She was calm now, knowing there was hope in the strength of Joel's heartbeat. She watched Markle intently as he took the rope from Joel's saddle horn and lashed him into the saddle. At last she was satisfied and permitted Markle to step back. He held his wounded arm and it dropped blood from his fingertips onto the trail.

'Start walking,' she said. 'And when you get to town tell Clay Harkman that Joel is still alive.' Her voice rose. 'And tell him a woman shot you. And if he wants Joel or me, tell him to come and get us!'

Markle stood a long moment. Finally he turned and started slowly down the pass toward the prairies. He looked back once to see her go to his gun and throw it into the river. He did not look back again but walked on.

She pushed Joel's gun back into his holster, mounted her own horse, took up the reins of Markle's and then rode to the ledge. She took the lantern in her hand and swung it wide. When she let it loose it arced out over the river. She heard it hiss as it hit the water and went out. That done, she headed her horse down the trail, leading the horse carrying Joel.

*   *   *

Markle was halfway to town and beginning to stumble from side to side on the road when he heard them coming. He called out his name and the riders pulled up sharply.

Wolf, in the lead, struck a match and leaned out of the saddle to look at Markle. 'What the hell?'

'No use,' Markle said. 'I got Lockhart, but Harkman's woman—his wife, she said—got me. She carted him off to Cardon's.

'Let a woman gun you down,' Wolf said contemptuously.

'No ordinary woman,' Markle said. 'Not a damned bit ordinary.' And he folded, knees first, into the road.

'Get him up.' Wolf ordered the others. 'Harkman can find some use for his carcass.' They put him behind the saddle, his head hanging off one side, his arms off the other.

Then they turned and rode for Lace Curtain.

*   *   *

A sharp burst of gunfire warned them as they reached town and Wolf led the way to the river. 'Not yet,' he said disgustedly. 'Harkman's got thirty men on that jailhouse and there's a half dozen holding them off.'

They followed the river path to the rear of

the saloon. Leaving Markle outside, still tied to the horse, they went inside.

Harkman was in his office, a cup of coffee, growing cold, on the desk beside him. Keno sat in a chair, his head down but his cold eyes wide awake.

'I sent you to find Markle,' Harkman snapped.

'Found him,' Wolf said. He told the story quickly.

Harkman heard him out, his hands pushed hard against the desk top.

'Then it was true what Red said,' Keno observed. 'It was your wife who hit him over the head and took out after Lockhart.'

'Who could have known,' Harkman half whispered. He could not comprehend this. 'She hates force,' he said aloud.

Keno laughed aloud. 'She must hate it bad! She runs after Lockhart, shouting his name on the streets. And she's probably out there now telling Cardon the boys are coming after him.'

Harkman rose, walking around his desk and coming to a halt before Keno. He bent forward so that the man's cold eyes could not escape his own gaze.

'We don't know that she told Cardon anything.'

'Wolf here said—'

Harkman's voice was very tight, very low. 'We don't know.'

Keno returned Harkman's stare, his thin

mouth curled. And then his contempt slipped to one side and he lowered his head.

'We don't know,' he agreed.

Harkman straightened. 'I'll take care of this. You see that the jailhouse gets over here.'

Leppy Gotch kicked open the door then, bringing Markle in his arms, holding him as if he were a hardwood floor.

Harkman said, 'Bring him in. We'll patch him up.'

'Some woman,' Leppy crooned. 'Some woman shot Seth.' He poured whiskey into the wound and wrapped it with a clean cloth. He touched Markle's cheek with the back of his hand. 'Hot,' he said.

'All right,' Harkman said, 'clear out now, all of you. Keno, you see that you get that jailhouse before daylight.'

'With what?' Keno demanded. 'There's three inside and an army outside. A fine army! That Reeves woman is shooting from the cupola on Teel's stable and a few farmers are scattered around using us for targets. We can't even crawl close enough to do any good.'

'Burn her out—the farmers will run then.'

'No! I'll not fight a woman.'

Their eyes met again and this time Keno did not look away. It was Clay Harkman who did, and he said, 'Do it your way. But do it.'

They went out, taking Leppy with them, and Harkman knelt beside Markle. A whiskey bottle in one hand, he pried open the loose-lipped mouth. After a moment the man's throat muscles contracted, swallowing. His eyes came half open and he began to gulp. Harkman pulled back the bottle.

Markle breathed deeply and opened his eyes wider. He finally focused on Harkman and he struggled to sit up.

'You'll live,' Harkman said. 'Now tell it.'

'Said she was your wife,' Markle muttered. He licked his slack lips. 'Gimme a drink.'

'Tell it!'

'By God, I got Lockhart just like you said. Skinned his head first shot and knocked him off his horse. When I heard him coming I was set at the pass. He came in slow but he was close enough and I furrowed him. I got the lantern and went to see—and she come riding up. Gimme a drink.'

Harkman brought a bottle of his own and pulled the cork. It was a flat pint so Markle could hold it easily in one hand. When he set it down it was a third empty and there was color in his face.

'Riding like a squaw,' he said. His voice was awed. 'Skirts tucked up and her hugging the saddle like she was born in it. And a gun in her hand. She says she's your wife and shoots me in the gun arm. She saw Lockhart was alive and made me get my horse and rope him to it. She took my gun and threw it in the creek. She was smart; she took his before she let me touch him. Then she told me to start walking and to tell you—' He broke off and lifted the bottle.

Harkman's eyes never left his face.

'She said, "Start walking, and when you get to town tell Clay Harkman that Joel is still alive. Tell him a woman shot you—and if he wants Joel or me to come and get us!" The very words,' Markle added. 'And it was a helluva walk.'

Harkman did not hear his complaint. He had turned and was walking to his desk. He sat down, dropping like a man with his strength run out. 'Joel,' he whispered. So that was the way of it! He wondered how long it had been going on—how much of it before they had come here. He laughed abruptly, harshly.

'She kept you from bringing in Lockhart,' he said.

Markle was sucking at the bottle, and he paused to rub it against his lips, 'Yeah, she did.'

'You owe her for that.'

Markle lifted his head and for an instant his watery eyes were clear with understanding. 'You still want Lockhart brought in?'

Clay Harkman stared at his hands. He spoke so that Markle could barely hear him. 'Just Lockhart,' he said.

Markle twisted the bottle, not taking his eyes from Harkman. He thought of the woman, and she was something vital and shining, and he could not comprehend the feeling. He thought of Harkman and he knew that without him he, Markle, was nothing. He could not give it words but Harkman's approval had always been his air and wine.

'Just Lockhart,' he repeated. 'Alive,' he added for himself. His head dropped but suddenly he tilted the bottle, letting the rest of the liquor slide down his throat. He threw the empty bottle aside with a crash.

'All right,' he said.

CHAPTER ELEVEN

As it grew lighter the gunfire in town ceased, dying out slowly until a final shot came from the west. At sunrise Abel Kine walked from the rear of the jailhouse and stood in full view.

'Good enough,' he called, and walked toward Sam Teel's.

'This is the best place to see from,' Elmira Reeves said from above. He went up to take her place, taking her rifle since he carried only a forty-four.

He checked the load in the rifle. 'Go get some rest. They ain't licked, but they'll stay quiet until dark, is my guess.'

She clambered down. The quiet was intense.

In the hotel she found Jed Hopper and Lem Happy seated at the table. Nora was by the stove making coffee. Elmira sat down and looked at the men.

'What was the ruckus in here last night?' For once there was no steam in her voice.

Nora answered from her place by the stove. 'Harkman's wife came over and rode after Joel.'

'It don't make sense,' Jed Hopper complained. 'Harkman's wife wouldn't stop Markle. He's Harkman's gun hand.'

'I ran to get you last night,' Nora said, 'but the shooting started and I had to come back.' She looked at them now with a faint glimmer of understanding in her eyes. 'I thought like you did, Jed, but—' She broke off to bring the coffee pot to the table. 'She was driven. She walked right into my rifle. It meant less than nothing to her. She loves Joel. It was in her voice.'

'I don't trust her,' Elmira said. She glanced toward her daughter. 'Because you're in love yourself, everything looks romantic. I don't trust it at all.'

'I don't know what happened to Lockhart and Markle,' Jed Hopper said, 'but I do know this town ain't the best place to be in right now.' He studied Elmira Reeves for some time, speaking more to her with his eyes than with words.

She shook her head, stubbornly. 'Yes,' Hopper said. 'We can fight better without you and Nora in the way.'

'And what if *that* woman is there?'

'From what it sounds to me,' Abel Kine said, coming in, 'I'd be proud to know her.' He pulled out a chair and dropped into it. 'I got the farmers watching.' He lit his stubby pipe. 'I been standing, listening,' he confessed cheerfully. 'I'll ride out to Cardon's with you, Elmira.'

'I'll not go,' she said stubbornly, but there was no conviction in her voice.

Kine grinned and looked away from her. 'Get me some coffee, honey,' he said to Nora. 'Shooting placer miners all night is plumb tuckering.'

* * *

Joel awakened to strangeness. He tried to lift himself and felt a sharp pain running up his left temple—then he remembered.

'Rode right into it,' he muttered. He called out, but his voice was a dry croak. He tried it again and made an appreciable noise, enough so he could hear footsteps stirring.

The room was dim with heavy burlap-bag curtains drawn over the window, and when the door opened it took him a moment to make out his sister. Behind her was Juanita Harkman.

'You,' he said. 'So it was you called to me.'

Her face was drawn, pale beneath the dusky tone of her skin, but as she came up to him he saw her eyes gladden. She stood by the bed, looking down but not speaking. He raised his hand from the cover and she took it in her slender fingers, holding it quietly.

Ellen Cardon went to the window and pinned back the curtains, letting in cold sunlight. When she came to the bed Juanita made a move as if to drop Joel's hand but Ellen shook her head.

'I'll get him something to eat,' she said.

Joel studied them both. 'You've changed your mind,' he said to his sister.

'I thank her for your life,' she answered. 'That's enough proof for me—and for Tim.'

When she had gone, Joel said, 'Don't stand.' Juanita released his hand long enough to draw forward a chair and, sitting, took his fingers in hers again. 'Where's Tim?' he asked.

'Guarding the pass against Clay's men,' she said. She looked down into his face, studying it. His eyelids drooped and raised again. She pushed back the chair. 'I'll let you sleep.'

'Not yet,' he said. He tried to draw her to him. She removed her hand gently. 'I'm still Clay Harkman's wife,' she said, and left him.

He slept and woke and slept again. When he roused himself the third time it was growing dark outside. There was a glass of water on the chair within reach of his hand. He drank thirstily, spilling water down his chin. Replacing the glass, he called out. He felt better and his voice was stronger.

Tim came into the room, shaking his head and grinning. He lighted a lamp and went to the window, dropping the curtains over it.

'You sure do things the hard way,' he said. He dropped into a chair and began to shape a cigarette. He gave it to Joel, rolled one for himself and then lighted them both.

'How about the pass?' Joel asked. He sucked smoke deeply, enjoying it.

'Abbey's guarding it,' Tim said. 'But I guess there's no need. Harkman's called a truce.'

'You can't trust that,' Joel said.

'Nothing we can do,' Tim said. 'And it gives us a breather.' He shifted in the chair. 'Elmira and Nora brought the news out. Jed made 'em come just like you figured.'

'It's safer—and better,' Joel said.

Tim made a point of studying his cigarette. 'Might be,' he agreed reluctantly. 'But it seems the woman—Juanita—hoorawed Nora some last night, and Elmira's not happy at her being here.' Joel waited, and finally Tim blurted out what he knew of Juanita's story.

'She did, that?' Joel said wonderingly. 'Then Harkman knows?'

'Seeing she turned Markle loose and he's in town, Harkman knows,' Tim admitted. 'But Elmira still doesn't trust her.'

'Natural,' Joel said. 'Hopper doesn't trust me —and for less reason.'

Tim got up. 'Ellen's readied some soup for you,' he said, and went out quickly.

Juanita came in, bringing the bowl of soup. She set it down on the chair and helped him to sit up. Then, handing him the soup, she sat down quietly, her hands folded in her lap. He spooned the soup to cool it.

'I hear there's a truce,' he said.

'I don't know what it means.'

He tasted the soup. It made him hungry and he ate steadily for a minute. Then the hunger was gone and he handed the half-empty bowl to her.

'You're keeping from saying things,' he told her.

She reached out, smoothing the pillow behind his head. 'Clay sent out word for me, she said. Her eyes met his and moved aside. 'My returning is part of the truce.'

'And you'll go?'

'I can't stay here,' she said. 'And if it means peace—I'll go.' She lifted her head. 'What can he do to me?'

'Peace? For whom? As long as I stay here, you can. You—' He broke off. 'Elmira?'

'Nothing has been said to me,' she answered quickly.

Women didn't have to say anything, he thought. They had ways that spoke more than words.

'You can't blame her,' Juanita said. 'I'd be the same. Things have been hard for her too long.'

He said, as if he hadn't heard her, 'But not

back to Harkman.'

'If I go, I may be able to stop Clay from doing more.'

He saw that she did not believe what she was saying. 'You told me yourself that nothing will stop him this time.' He took her hand. 'I want your promise.'

'That I stay?'

'That you'll not go to him.' She stared down soberly and, with a rough motion, he pulled her to him, releasing her hand and slipping an arm about her shoulders, bringing her mouth to his. She went to her knees and cradled his head gently in her arms, her lips now warm and yielding.

'You think,' he said, 'I could let you go after what you did?'

She rocked back. 'I must help. I can't do anything here.'

'You might teach Nora Reeves to use a rifle that she has aimed at somebody,' he said with an attempt at lightness.

'So I might,' she said soberly. 'She doesn't dislike me for what I did, you know. She understands —her mother doesn't.'

Joel thought of what Nora had told him about Jed Hopper. 'It will come,' he said. 'Give it time.'

Bending, she kissed him quickly. 'Sleep a while,' she said, and went into the other room.

Her kiss kept him from remembering until too late that she had not given him her promise.

They were in the kitchen around the table and she stepped to the far end and seated herself. 'He's much better,' she said.

Ellen smiled. 'Enough to muss your hair,' she said without meanness. 'Now you'd better eat, too.'

Juanita felt Elmira Reeves' heavy disapproval, but there was nothing said and she began to eat. They were all quiet and she realized it was because of her presence. Only Elmira was against her, she knew, but still they disliked talking about Clay when she was in the room.

She said, 'If I go, will Clay keep to his truce?'

Kine answered her. 'No. It's like the jailhouse. If we give it to him, then he'll be after something else. The more he gets, the more he'll want. He's just buzzing like a horsefly—to keep us occupied.'

'Maybe until he gets the miners in here,' Tim said. 'If the news of that gold strike spreads, he'll have five hundred more voters.'

'Voters!' Kine snorted. 'He's got fifty miners now who'll swap a vote for a shot of rotten whiskey. There never was any principle to a placer miner. No, it ain't time to get men here he wants. I only wish I knew what it was.'

A silence fell and Juanita was conscious of Elmira Reeves' accusing stare. She knew what Elmira was thinking—that she, Juanita, should know what Clay would do next, and that she should tell them.

She rose. 'Perhaps Joel would like a cup of coffee,' she said. Getting it, she left the room.

She stood before Joel's door for some time. She realized that she did know why Clay had called the truce, and why one of his terms had been her return. That was the real reason—he had to have her back safely before he could go ahead.

He was afraid she would tell them the one thing that could destroy him. And yet, didn't he know that as long as she was his wife, it was the one thing she could not tell? Until that phase of her life was ended, she would do nothing.

She stood with one hand lightly on the door latch. Finally, she set the cup on the floor and turned away. She went to Ellen's room and lit a lamp.

From a drawer of the dresser she took a heavy scarf and wrapped it about her hair. There were shells from Tim's gun on the dresser and after checking to see that they matched her gun, she put them in her pocket.

Without further hesitation, she blew out the lamp, slid up the window and slipped into the night.

When she neared the pass she could see Abbey sitting silently on guard, a cigarette coal the only sign that he was awake. He had come upright at the sounds she made and she called out to reassure him.

'It's Juanita Harkman,' she said.

Abbey struck a match. 'On foot!'

'Joel would have taken a horse and followed,' she explained. She did not know Abbey well, but there was something about the man, a slight hesitance in his manner, that she did not trust. So, she said only, 'I'm going back to Clay.'

'With the plans?' Abbey asked sharply.

'I don't know any plans,' she said. 'And I won't betray anyone—neither Clay nor Joel. Let me by.'

He dropped the match and stepped back. 'You can tell him the pass is well guarded. He can come through under truce but no other way.'

'I'll tell him nothing,' she said, and walked on.

The last half mile into town she had followed the river path, reaching the saloon by the rear. There were no lights, no sounds as she walked slowly up the stairs and down the hall to his office. She pushed open the door and listened. From the other room she could hear the small noise he made while sleeping, and she stepped in, shutting the door behind her.

A streak of early morning came in through the front windows. It was enough to show her her own baggage piled in the center of the room. She turned from it and went to the sofa that lay along the wall opposite the door to his room. It was cold but she was too weary to care, and she lay down fully clothed. After a moment she sat up and pulled off her shoes. They were nearly worn through and there were holes in her stockings. She thought about replacing them with others from her small bag but she lacked the energy. Pulling off Ellen Cardon's scarf, she lay back, tucking the gun beneath the sofa pillow she rested on.

With the memory of Joel's kiss, she fell quietly asleep.

*   *   *

Harkman roused after sunrise and washed and dressed before going into his office. He opened the door wide and stepped in. The door remained open while he stared, motionless, at the sofa. Then he shut the door silently and tiptoed toward the hall.

'Clay!'

He swung around, like a man on a pivot. She was sitting up, the gun in her hand. 'Put that away,' he said contemptuously.

'I can use it,' she said. 'Ask Markle.' He started toward her. 'And I will. Go sit down, Clay.' Her voice was steady but inside she was feeling the impact of this first real rebellion against him.

'I don't understand this, Juanita.' He made a move to go to his desk, but her voice halted him sharply.

'Take a chair where I can watch you.'

Shrugging, he sat across from her. 'May I smoke?'

She ignored his sarcasm. 'If you wish,' she said, and watched him closely until he had taken a cigar from his pocket. 'I came to tell you something, Clay. There will be no more of this.'

'Of what, Juanita?'

'Of men like Markle,' she said. 'Of warring—of your trampling and crushing.' Never before had she spoken to him quite like this. But his open amazement gave her courage, and she rushed on.

'I have the power to stop you, Clay. Don't smile—you know it's true. That's why you made your truce—to get me back. I've been at Cardon's nursing Joel Lockhart, but I haven't told them anything yet. I haven't told them what I can—what I will.'

'What you will?' he repeated.

'I came to tell you first, Clay. To give you the chance to stop—now.'

'Ah, the chance.'

She stood, brushing a strand of hair back from her forehead but never letting the gun waver from him. 'Go away,' she said. She hesitated, but she must be fair. She must give him all the chance she could as her husband. 'We'll go together.'

His eyes met hers strongly, hitting her like a

physical blow. 'Away! Start over—start over again?' He lifted a hand and stared at it. 'All my life I've waited for this chance, and you want me to throw it away. For what? Your feelings?'

'Life,' she said. 'Human life and decency.'

'What are a few lives?' he demanded. 'What is decency? It will come—more and greater. My way will bring it where theirs won't. It has always been the best way, through history. It will always be that way. The strong over the weak. The strong to lead the weak.'

'The weak together can be strong,' she said softly. 'But I won't argue, Clay. This stops and we go away, or I tell them what I know—and with that they can stop you.'

'You would do this?' he asked.

She saw that he still did not believe. 'Give me your answer, Clay.'

'Tell them anything you wish,' he said rashly.

'Then,' she said almost sadly, 'I no longer consider myself your wife. I had to give you your chance first. But now I'm free to do as I wish.'

'Now you're free!' He threw back his head and laughed. 'No one is free. And do you think anything you could tell them would change things—now?' He swept his hand through the air and she could see the belief in his power, riding over his face.

Without removing her eyes from him, she

bent and picked up her smallest bag. She backed to the door, set down the bag, and fumbled the key from the lock. She opened the door, pushed the bag into the hall with her foot, and stepped out.

'Wait! It's Lockhart, isn't it?'

'It's many things, Clay. It's ten years of greed and ambition and cruelty. But it's Lockhart now too.'

She got the door shut and locked before his shoulder struck the panel with jarring force. She could hear his hoarse breathing, almost a smothered cry. She shook her head and, picking up the bag, started down the stairs, into the saloon.

Keno was there, staring open-mouthed at the sight of her. She was in her stocking feet, her dress torn and stained from her night's ride and her long walk, her hair half loose. But she carried herself proudly as she walked to the door.

Seth Markle, one arm in a sling, stood by the bar, and he turned to watch her. There was no one else in the room.

'Clay's in his office,' she said. 'I think he'll want you both.' She faced them, her gun held in readiness, and backed out the door.

She walked into the bright sunshine, crossed the street and went up to the hotel. She stopped by the desk. Jed Hopper was behind it, staring at her with suspicion on his face. She laid down the gun, butt first, and dropped her bag.

'I'd like my room back,' she said.

'Your husband wants you,' he blurted out.

'No,' she said. 'Clay Harkman wants me—or he will soon. But he's no longer my husband. I just told him so.'

'With that?' Hopper asked, touching the gun.

'With that,' she said. 'It's the only language he can hear now.'

'Ah,' Jed said. He picked up the gun, took a key from the rack, and came around for her bag. She followed him up the stairs and into her room. He sat down the bag, put the gun on the dresser, and handed her the key.

Without speaking, he shut the door on her and went down the stairs. He heard the lock click behind him and then the bedsprings make a protest as she lay down.

At the foot of the stairs he paused to light a pipe. He tossed the match aside and went into a small room off the kitchen. 'Lem,' he said, and the old man rose from a cot. 'Harkman's wife—used to be his wife—is here. It might be a good idea to figure what he plans to do about her.'

Lem Happy stretched and giggled. 'It ain't dark yet,' he said.

'I don't think we got till dark,' Hopper told him.

*   *   *

It was barely dusk when the hammering on the door drove Juanita away from sleep. She sat up in bed, blinking, and then remembering. She called out, 'Yes?'

'Kine out here.'

She rose and unlocked the door. Returning to the bed, she sat up with the covers pulled to her chin. She told him to come in.

He burst into the room, blurting, 'You blamed idiot—ma'am.' He stopped, flushing.

'How is Joel?' she asked.

'Joel's all right. He's safe. It's you that ain't. He's snorting and rearing around like a stabbed steer. Now get dressed and come on.'

'I'm all right here,' she said.

'Maybe so,' he answered. 'But Jed ain't. Lem Happy come loping out to Cardon's with the news not two hours ago. Harkman's going to raid this place—to get you.'

She should have known. But weariness had clogged her mind. 'And if I go to Cardon's, he'll find a way to get me there,' she said.

'You ain't going to Cardon's,' he said. 'I kept that idiot Joel in bed by promising I'd see to you. And I will.' He glared indignantly at her. 'You're coming with me.'

She felt a sudden warmth for this man. 'Why do you do this?'

'No time,' he said brusquely. 'Ma'am, I'm an old bachelor but I'll pull you out of that bed as you be if you don't come and come quick.'

She smiled. 'Give me five minutes.'

He slammed out of the room.

She opened her bag and laid clothing on the bed. She shook her head. Shoes and stockings, yes, but a skirt was too much of an encumbrance. A woman was a woman, but there was a time when it was an unhandy thing to be.

'Mr. Kine,' she called, 'get me a shirt and trousers from Joel's room, please.'

She was dressed to the point of needing them when he eased the door open slightly and threw them into the room. The trousers were long, but not too much, since he was narrower in the hips than she. His shirt was large, too, but it was warm and comfortably loose. She finished her dressing by twisting Ellen's scarf about her hair. Tucking Clay's gun into the waistband of Joel's trousers, she walked into the hall.

Kine said only, 'Good,' and led her at a quick pace to the kitchen and out to the rear yard. A drooping mule stood saddled beside a small dun mare. Kine helped her onto the mare and adjusted her stirrups.

A gun went off by the jailhouse and another across the street from the hotel. Lem Happy appeared around the corner of the building, blowing smoke from his rifle.

'You're cut off,' he said. 'They're all over the road.'

'Didn't want to go that way nohow,' Kine

said. He started his mule south, toward the Reeves' house. Behind it a small cut angled out of the cliff face and he led Juanita in there.

'Steep,' he warned her. 'We got to walk the animals up.'

From behind them the cracking of rifles was plain but as they led the horses up the slender thread of trail along the rock face the sounds grew fainter. Soon Kine led her over a hump, and they dipped into a cup rimmed by pines and firs.

'We ride from here,' he said. 'My claim's back a piece.'

She heard a last, faint gunshot. 'If Clay knew I was gone—'

'He'll know soon enough,' Kine said. 'But it won't stop him now. He's using everything he's got this time.'

They rode on, the twilight deepening as the forest grew thicker about them. Once they stopped, resting their horses on a bare ridge above the treetops. Kine looked back and his half-swallowed curse swung Juanita around. A great glow tinted the darkening western sky, reaching up to flat, thickening clouds.

'God a'mighty,' he said. 'Harkman's fired the hotel!'

CHAPTER TWELVE

Lem happy, in the loft of Reeves' store, broke for the hotel when the first faint flames licked at the roof.

Jed Hopper yelled down from the cupola on the blacksmith shop but his voice was lost in a burst of gunfire. He saw the old man stagger and fall flat, rise and fall again.

Hopper began to swear and tears of helplessness mixed with his words.

'We wasn't ready,' Hopper said over and over. 'I told 'em we wasn't ready.'

The flames on the hotel roof were taking a stronger hold. A section of the roof caved in and the walls caught, roaring with the fury of dry wood.

'To hell with it!' Hopper cried. He crawled down from the cupola and ran, staggering in his limping haste, across the rear yard to the old man.

A shot spit dirt at his feet and he threw his rifle away to show them he was through. He reached Happy behind the store and he knelt. The old man was breathing hoarsely. A fleck of blood spotted his beard and Hopper wiped it away.

'Where you hit?'

'They burned our hotel, Jed.'

'We'll build us another. Where you hit?'

'Brisket,' the old man said.

They rode up, surrounding Hopper, and he let them take him. It was too late to move Happy and so he had to let him lie. Hopper went off to the jailhouse, his game leg dragging. He sat in the dark, not even bothering when they hitched teams to the building and snaked it across the street and alongside the saloon.

He heard Harkman's voice and the voices of some of the farmers and he knew they had given up. He stood and limped to the cell window. They were standing by the front of the saloon, their arms raised.

'Go on home, boys,' he called out to them. 'It's all done.'

'Go home and pack,' Harkman said. 'There'll be no more farming in this valley.'

Jed Hopper stood at the window, watching them ride off, in the light of the flames from the hotel. When they were out of sight he stared curiously at the burning hotel until the last wall crumpled and then he returned to the cot and lowered himself onto it.

'We wasn't ready,' he said. 'I knew we wasn't ready.'

* * *

At daybreak, Harkman roused his men. With Keno flanking him and Wolf riding behind with Leppy Gotch, he took the road to the valley at a steady lope. When a voice rang out from the top of Whispering Canyon, Harkman reined in, signaling his men to do the same.

He rode forward, leaving them out of earshot, and pulled up a few feet from the man on guard. 'Coming under truce,' he said.

Abbey stepped into view, a rifle cradled in his arm. 'Come for what reason?'

Harkman let his voice carry back, loudly. 'For my wife.'

Abbey shook his head. 'She went out night before last.'

'And came back in,' Harkman said. 'Kine brought her back.'

'Not through here,' Abbey said.

'Then over the mountains. What difference does it make?'

'Just this.' Abbey propped the rifle against his leg and fashioned a cigarette. He talked in a low tone, his head down so that he seemed to be concentrating on making his smoke.

'Lockhart's up and around.' His tongue licked the paper. 'He's in love with her.'

'I know,' Harkman said impatiently.

'He'll stop you from finding her if you ride in this way.'

'He can try,' Harkman said.

Abbey struck a match and inhaled smoke. 'There'll be no breaking of the truce or you don't go through.'

Harkman laughed at him. 'No breaking of the truce,' he agreed. 'Not this trip. But give me an hour. I'm coming back alone.'

Abbey dropped his match and twisted his boot toe on it. He picked up the gun and faded back over the bank of the trail. Harkman signaled his men and they rode up and past the summit.

'Easy,' Keno commented dryly.

'Why not?' Harkman said. 'There's still a truce.'

'Unless Kine and the woman got through to Cardon's.'

'We'll see,' Harkman said. 'We'll see when we get there.'

At Cardon's they came in wide, making sure they were seen. Tim and Joel were standing by the rear door, waiting. Joel wore a heavy bandage and no hat. His face was drawn but he stood without support.

'I came for my wife,' Harkman said.

'I'm looking for her myself,' Joel told him quietly.

Harkman made an angry gesture toward his gun but Keno clamped a hand on his arm. 'They've got guns on you from the house.'

Harkman put both hands over his saddle horn, squeezing down hard. 'I came to tell you all to pack and go. You're through here. Next time I show up I'll have fifty men.

'Bring 'em,' Tim Cardon offered. 'Now I'll give you two minutes to get off my land.'

'Until tomorrow,' Harkman warned flatly. He wheeled his horse and rode north, his men following, until they were out of sight over a roll in the grasslands. There Harkman signaled a halt.

'Kine hasn't been here,' he said. 'That means he's got her somewhere in the hills. Keno, you take Leppy and see if you can't locate his place.' He waved them off and they went east, swinging wide so as not to be seen by Cardon when they were ready to cut into the bank of hills on the south.

Wolf spat as Harkman said, 'You go to Lost Hole and get ready to drive the stock back. We'll move them in as soon as Cardon gets out.'

'You think Cardon's scared out?'

'Ride,' Harkman said. 'I know what I'm doing.' He looked steadily at Wolf. 'And keep in sight of Cardon's place as much as possible.'

Wolf opened his mouth in surprise, shut it and grinned. Harkman watched him go, keeping to the high places where he would attract the most attention. He nodded in satisfaction and headed back for the pass.

He found Abbey waiting. 'I ordered Cardon out by tomorrow,' he said.

'I'm not going,' Abbey told him.

'No need,' Harkman said. 'Hopper's in jail. The farmers are pulling out today. The valleys are yours.'

'Lockhart?' Abbey asked. His eyes met Harkman's. 'Your wife?'

'Kine has her. Keno and Gotch are out

hunting.'

'Kine is too clever for them.'

'I think Lockhart knows where she is,' Harkman said. 'And that's what I want you for.' He spoke quickly, telling Abbey about Wolf. 'If Lockhart knows where she is, you can follow him and find out. If he doesn't, then he'll track Wolf to Lost Hole.'

'And then?'

'And then,' Harkman said slowly, 'we have him.'

Abbey nodded, as if only half hearing. 'So you've got the town.'

'I've got the town. I said, follow Lockhart.'

'I'll do it,' Abbey said.

Harkman studied him a moment and then he held one palm up, open, and squeezed it slowly shut. 'I've got it now,' he said. 'It's mine—and yours. You made the right choice.'

'It's nothing to be proud of,' Abbey said.

'All this land,' Harkman pointed out. 'You can build a house in the middle of it. That's a fine thing to offer a wife, Abbey.'

'Get riding,' Abbey said. 'I'm paying for it. Every foot of it.'

Harkman started off and then twisted in the saddle. 'When Cardon is down, Wolf will bring the cattle—your cattle—down from Lost Hole.' He rode off, his horse's hooves ringing on the rock floor of the pass.

Abbey studied the ground, not watching him. The soft wind whispered in his ears. He lifted his head. 'I'll do it,' he muttered. 'I'll do it!'

Harkman rode on to town, feeling his power as strongly as he felt the surge of his horse's stride. Let them cry.

'Sheep!' he said aloud.

Juanita came to his mind and he tasted a moment of bitterness.

'She can't do anything,' he said. But the shadow of what she knew still lay, covering every picture he created. He had to get her before she slipped away and told her story. She still had the power to destroy him.

When he reached town the hotel was smoking rubble and ashes. The only life seemed to be the creaking of a wagon as the first farmer started his journey south. He was up by the jailhouse, drooped on the wagon seat with his wife beside him. His goods were piled high on the box and two children rode on top, as silent as their parents.

Harkman was close behind when Jed Hopper called from the jailhouse window. The farmer stood up to hear better.

'Keep in touch,' Hopper said.

Harkman, laughed shortly. 'Move on. There's no more room here—ever.'

The man sat down, his shoulders sagging. Past the jailhouse, he turned, standing again, as if to get a last look at his land. And then he faced south and kept that way until he was out of sight.

Harkman rode over to the blacksmith shop and Sam Teel came out at his call, a sledge in one thick hand. He spat tobacco juice onto the ground and looked inquiringly at Harkman.

'All the shoeing is across the street from now on,' Harkman said. 'We'll move you today.'

Teel scratched his head and spat again. He looked at the jailhouse and then let his eyes travel south down the road where the farmer's wagon had gone.

'I like it well enough here,' he said mildly.

'I said we move you today, Teel.'

Sam Teel studied the ground and then looked again at the jailhouse. He could see Hopper at the bars, the sunlight casting a ribbed pattern across his face.

'What's the difference between me and him if I move?' he asked.

'A smart man goes where the business is,' Harkman said.

Teel saw Markle come onto the jailhouse porch. He carried a rifle in his good arm and he wore a deputy's star on his shirt front. Teel sighed heavily and shifted his hammer to his other hand long enough to wipe sweat from his palm. He gripped the hammer again and studied the sky. It was a fine blue today. He lowered his gaze to Jed Hopper and he spat once more.

'Reckon,' he said, 'I'll stay where I am,' and he flung the hammer at Harkman.

Markle's gun made a swift, cracking sound in the quiet daylight. Harkman leaned to one side, feeling the hammer graze his shoulder.

Teel was thrown back against the shop wall. He clung to it, staring down at the blood welling from his chest.

'Some men,' he said 'get off the fence too late.' He pitched forward on his face and lay still.

* * *

After Wolf was out of sight, Tim and Joel returned to the house. Ellen came down from the attic with Nora and Elmira Reeves behind her. Ellen sat her rifle in the kitchen corner.

'Keno and Leppy Gotch rode east and swung into the hills,' Ellen said.

'Wolf went in about the same direction,' Tim told her.

'Harkman sent them after her,' Joel said. He dropped into a chair.

'Kine's got her,' Tim told him. 'You needn't worry as long as Kine has her.'

'Worry? Harkman will hunt until she's found,' Joel said. 'If she went to him and left again, then she told him she was through. She's like that, Tim. She would tell him first.'

'Tell him what?' Tim swung around the room. 'What is there to tell—that she loves you?'

'That she'll use what she knows against him

now,' Joel said. 'There is something—but she wouldn't tell me before. And Harkman will want her shut up. It was on his face that he fears her.'

Tim paced the room restlessly, studying it. He swung to Joel. 'All right, when do we start?'

'I, not we,' Joel said. He rose. 'You've got a home to defend.'

'Against an army,' Tim said bitterly.

'At the pass,' Joel reminded him. 'If they start through, dynamite it.' He went into the other room, getting extra shells for his gun and his warm coat. His sister caught him at the doorway.

'You can't go alone.' He struggled into his coat and she went on, 'I should have shot him when I had the chance.'

'We aren't murderers,' Joel said. 'He came under a truce. When he does come to fight, then draw your bead fine.'

Tim went with him to the barn and saddled the close-coupled black Joel liked.

'Luck,' he said briefly, and turned aside.

Joel rode east along the edge of the hills until he cut the sign of the three riders. All of them had joined at a point out of sight of the house and he had no trouble following the trail they made. It led into a narrow-mouthed draw that sloped upward almost at once. Joel came out suddenly on a sharp ridge and stopped to blow his horse.

He started again, following the still-plain

sign. The trail dipped down and then up into a second canyon. As he rode, the walls began to narrow abruptly, their slopes covered with pine and cedar and occasionally a tamarack, straight and bare and towering over the others.

Without warning, the trail broke over the top of a heavily timbered flat. It was scarcely more than a ledge on the hillside and he could see the canyon continuing on his left. Here the trail forked, one branch toward the canyon, and the other, a lighter marking, to his right into the timber.

He studied the sign with care. Two of the men, one of them heavy on his horse, had ridden to the right. Leppy Gotch and Keno, he thought. The other man, Wolf probably, had gone left on a more heavily used trail.

He kept in the new canyon, swallowed by its steep slopes that cut off the sun. The floor was flat and at one place a spring oozed out of rock and crossed it. An old windfall lay here at an angle and had formed a dam so that there was a pool of water behind it. The clear prints of a single horse lay in the mud around the pool.

He pushed on. The canyon continued to twist upward, widening all the time, until he broke onto a second flat. The main trail was easily seen and he continued along it, going south now, until he realized it had faded out.

The ground here was frozen and rocky so that all markings were obscured. He was high enough so that a few patches of snow lay beneath the trees and the air had a bite to it. He retraced his steps until he picked up the last clear sign. He started up again more slowly, but the ground was too hard to carry prints. He tried a draw that opened to his left and reached a dead end of sheer rock. He went out and up the main trail again. A second draw and a third ended as the first, blocked by cliff faces. The fourth ran a stream of clear water over heavy gravel and he halted to let his horse drink.

He dismounted and knelt upstream from the horse to have a drink himself. As he straightened, he saw a cigarette butt lying on the rock beside his hand. He touched it with a probing finger and found it fresh. He mounted again and followed the stream until the walls on either side became steep and bare and the water filled the canyon floor. He was ready to turn back when he saw cattle sign where the last of the gravelly beach shelved into water.

He put his horse into the stream and followed it. The water wasn't over a foot deep anywhere but a sharp current made the going hard for the little black. Ahead the stream turned into what seemed to be a wall of solid rock. But, reaching it, Joel found a small falls and, beyond, a marshy meadow that lay cupped between high bluffs. A heavy drift of snow lay at the far end. He plodded through the meadow, filled with last year's dead grass, but churned and trampled more than any pack string could manage. The snow, when he reached it, was muddied by many hooves, and he halted again.

The hoofprints were definitely those of cattle and he was certain now that this trail could not lead to Kine's. The remembrance of the Lost Hole Tim and Abbey had mentioned came to him and he turned back. He could remember the trail and so tell Tim, he thought, but there was no time now to hunt for rustled stock.

He put the horse back over the falls and into the stream, reining for the sharp turn when a horse and rider came around it and a rifle butt swung for his head. He cried out but it was too late. The rifle caught him alongside the chin, driving him out of the saddle and into the water.

* * *

Abbey kept his distance, letting Joel disappear over one hummock before he rose from behind the one shielding himself.

At the turn in the creek, he stopped his horse and slid off. He crept up to the falls and raised himself so he could see the meadow. Joel was ahead, studying the snowdrift. When he swung back, Abbey ducked down and crawled back to his horse. He climbed on and took his rifle by the barrel. He was ready when the sound of water splashing told him Joel's horse had reached the creek. He spurred forward, rounding the turn, the rifle swinging. He saw the look of amazement on Joel's face.

Joel cried out, 'Abbey!' and went down under the swinging gun.

Abbey pushed his rifle into the saddle boot and swung down into the water. He dragged Joel into the meadow and knelt, feeling for his heart.

'No damage done,' he said to himself, and was surprised to find relief easing the sudden shaking of his muscles.

He caught Joel's horse and roped Joel into the saddle. That done, he mounted again and rode to the snowdrift and through it. Just beyond, over the brow of a slope, a trail went down abruptly. Abbey eased himself up to the top and looked over. Lost Hole lay below, a vast, flat-bottomed cup, protected on all sides by high walls. Green grass faded into the distance and the only snow was along the edges where the sun seldom reached. Cattle grazed just at the base of the trail and a long shack was beside it, smoke coming slowly from a stovepipe chimney.

Abbey saw that Joel was tight in the saddle and then quirted his horse, sending him down the trail toward the log house below. He swung his own horse around and rode away fast, back to the warm sunshine of his valley.

CHAPTER THIRTEEN

Joel awakened to the sour smell of unwashed men penned into an airless room. He was on a bunk and when he raised his head he could see a good deal around him.

He remembered Abbey coming at him from around the turn in the creek, and the swinging rifle. And that was all. Now he was here, in what must be Lost Hole, and he could only have come with Abbey's help.

He shut his eyes. His head throbbed from his wound and from the rifle butt that had raised a swelling on his chin.

He slept for a time and when he woke the pain had lessened to a slow, steady pulsating. He sat up carefully. After a minute, he swung his legs over the edge of the bunk and lowered himself to a rough board floor. A few deep breaths and he turned toward the front. He focused his eyes in the dusk and began walking carefully forward. He saw his gun and holster hanging over a chair by the long table and he made his way toward them.

A man rose from a chair by the stove, materializing out of shadow.

'Take a rest,' he said. 'You looked better when we drug you in.' He laughed at his own humor, showing Joel a toothless mouth. But the gun he held was steady enough and Joel stopped.

He dropped to the edge of the nearest bunk. The man went to the door, throwing it wide.

'Wolf, this 'un's awake.'

Wolf walked in, and bent forward, peering at Joel.

'So he is,' he said. 'We'll ride then.'

'Ride? Dump him here. We ain't staying.' The man laughed again. 'Let him homestead it.'

'Harkman wants him,' Wolf said. 'For bait.' He grinned and picked up Joel's gun and belt. 'This might make a good plant sometime, Ritchie,' he added, and threw the gun and belt at the other man.

Outside, Wolf ordered him on the black and then passed a rope around his legs, cinching them into the stirrups. He roped Joel's wrists to the saddle horn with painful tightness. A dozen men, strangers to Joel, stood by watching.

Wolf swung in the saddle. 'Get 'em rounded up tomorrow,' he said. 'We're making the drive as soon as Cardon's cleared out of the valley.'

He led the way up the trail, Ritchie coming up as a rear guard. Joel's gun and belt hung tantalizingly to his saddle horn and when Joel looked back at him, he grinned and indicated them.

The sun was completely gone even from the mountaintops by the time they reached the creek and Wolf was feeling his way when they reached the forks in the trail.

Wolf took the branch of the trail Keno and Leppy Gotch had followed, obviously thinking it safer to go through heavy timber than across the flats and run into Cardon.

In the darkness, Joel began to twist at the ropes on his wrists. He was counting on some give or looseness in the saddle horn and, when he found none, bent forward to work at the knots with his teeth. He was getting slack when Wolf reined up and drew him forward by hauling on the lead rope.

'Close in,' Wolf ordered. 'It's too dark to string out.'

It was harder now, but Joel worked on the slack ropes as well as he could. It was slow, agonizing work. Finally, one hand came free, blood oozing from his wrist where he had forced it from under the rope. With that much done, the rest was easy.

They started down a steep grade toward the prairie stretching westward. By the time they reached the valley floor and had swung toward Lace Curtain Joel's feet were loose enough to kick out of the stirrups.

Behind him, Ritchie hummed a doleful tune but Joel knew better than to expect the man to be off guard. He turned in the saddle, making an effort of it as if he were still roped tightly.

'Ritchie!' His voice was low, carried back by the wind of their movement. Ritchie began to edge up until he was only a few feet behind

Joel's horse. 'How much?' Joel asked.

Ritchie laughed, and Wolf slowed up ahead. 'What's that?'

'He maybe wants to buy a knife from me,' Ritchie said, and trotted up, keeping a few feet between himself and Joel. 'Shall I sell him one?'

'Keep an eye on him,' Wolf ordered.

Joel could wait no longer. He threw one leg over his saddle and used the foot still in the stirrup for a springboard. His thrust carried him away from the horse and out, onto Ritchie. The man yelled and then Joel had a grip with his arms, one of them around his neck that cut off his wind.

Joel freed one arm and brought Ritchie's head down with the other. His fist drove in, smashing Ritchie's nose and blinding him.

He heard Wolf coming and he let loose of Ritchie and grabbed for his gun hanging on the horn. He triggered twice and heard Wolf's horse neigh shrilly. Wolf shot and his bullet went high as his horse stumbled and crashed down.

Ritchie made a blinded, clawing motion at him and Joel laid the barrel hard against Ritchie's head, tumbling him half from the saddle. Wolf was on his feet. He shot again as Ritchie's horse bolted by him and Joel fired at the blast of his gun. Wolf cried out and Joel fired again. The horse reared, throwing Ritchie, and Joel got the reins and sawed him to a standstill.

He went over to Ritchie. But the man was out, stunned by his fall. Joel took the reins of Ritchie's horse and walked back until he found Wolf on the ground, kneeling as if in prayer, his forehead and arm resting on the altar made by his dying horse. Joel touched him and he slid to one side. Striking a match, Joel saw the great hole in the horse's neck. He shot the animal between the eyes.

His own horse was straining at the lead rope. Joel quieted him and got aboard. Slapping Ritchie's mount with the tip of his reins, he sent the horse galloping away north. Then he turned and rode toward town.

When he was almost at Lace Curtain, he left the road and hugged the hillside. The only lights were those in the saloon and he almost stumbled into the smoldering ashes of the hotel before he realized where he was.

He sat his horse in the dim starlight and stared at the gaunt finger of rock chimney that was the only thing still standing. The smell of charred wood was strong in his nostrils and a light breeze whipped rank smoke about him.

He rode around the remains of the hotel to the horse barn. It still stood and he left the horse tied in shadow by the door and continued on foot. He stumbled once on soft dirt behind the Miner's Supply and he knelt, feeling the mound until he understood its meaning.

'Whose grave?' he wondered, and walked on.

He passed the store and looked for Teel's. There was nothing but blackness stretching toward the hills southward. He looked across the street and saw the jailhouse and Teel's shop side by side, faintly outlined by the lights from the saloon.

He walked on south some distance before he crossed the road and turned back. He came to the side of Teel's shop and stopped in the shadow of its rear corner.

Twenty feet away someone called from the jailhouse porch to the saloon, 'Tell Leppy to get out here. I'm going in for a drink.' A match flared and Joel caught the profile of Seth Markle.

Soon the heavy footsteps of Leppy Gotch came clearly and Markle stepped toward the street. 'I need a drink,' he said.

'I'll watch,' Leppy said. 'You eat, too, Seth.' He spoke with the tone he might have used to a favorite child.

Joel took advantage of the noise made by their talking and broke rapidly for the rear of the jail building. He hauled up short past the corner, breathing softly.

'This is foolishness,' Markle's voice came clearly. 'There ain't no way for Hopper to get out.'

'Someone might steal him,' Leppy said.

'Hell,' Markle laughed, 'there ain't nobody

left to steal him.'

Joel smiled coldly in the darkness. So Hopper was inside! The sound of a horse thudding toward town wiped the smile from his lips. A man's voice raised in a hoarse shout:

'Keno! Get Keno. Lockhart's loose!'

Markle swore loudly, and the saloon doors banged open. Keno's gravelly voice was loud. 'What's this?'

'Me and Wolf was bringing in Lockhart,' Ritchie said excitedly. 'He clubbed me and killed Wolf. He must have turned my horse loose because the old fool came back to me.'

'I should have tied him,' Joel thought, and cursed a horse that could love a man like Ritchie. He could hear men pouring out of the saloon and above their noise came the sound of Harkman's voice. Joel stepped toward the rear door of the jailhouse and a man loomed up.

Joel drew his gun and hammered down, feeling it meet bone. The man became a dead weight against him and, when he stepped aside, fell forward into the weeds. Joel stooped, getting his gun from limp fingers, and pushed into the room.

'Jed?' he called softly.

Noise boiled up from outside, then quieted as Harkman's calm voice steadied the men. To Joel's right, Hopper said, 'Here.'

Joel turned, feeling bars. He thrust the gun through them and it was jerked from his hand.

'Markle's got the key,' Hopper said.

'No time,' Joel answered. 'Stand back.' The flare of a match showed him the lock and he fired into it. The roar was loud in the small space.

Hopper swung open the door and limped after Joel to the rear. Joel said, 'Hit for the river,' and they raced into darkness as someone broke through from the front. A gun crashed behind them and then men poured from the rear of the saloon. Another gun went off and the bullet whined past them into the water.

They followed the tree-lined bank until they were beyond Cobble's deserted cabin and reached high ground behind the next shack. They cut back toward the street and someone shouted: 'Don't shoot, damn it.'

Hopper chuckled and Joel pulled him forward across the empty space into the alley between two abandoned buildings. There were still shouts, some coming closer, but none to show they had been seen in their last quick run through darkness.

'I'm beat,' Hopper panted.

Joel took time to load his gun. 'Your horse?'

'In the barn—if it ain't burned.'

'It stands,' Joel said. 'Where's Happy?'

'Behind the Miner's Supply,' Hopper said bitterly. 'He was trying to save the hotel. Teel's where they left him—in his shop. He clumb off the fence straight at Harkman. Markle got him.'

Bootsteps sounded behind them. A man was coming cautiously up the alley. Joel drew back and when the man came abreast he slashed out with his gun. The man twisted, catching the blow on the shoulder. He cried out in alarm before Joel's next swing drove him to the ground.

'Come on,' Joel said, and they ran for the street. They were nearly to the far sidewalk before they were seen.

A voice shouted and a shot cracked out. It shattered the window of Reeves' store as they darted between it and the Miner's Supply. They swung into the yard and headed for the horse barn.

'Take my horse,' Joel panted. 'And tell Tim that Abbey knows where Lost Hole is.' He told the story briefly as he helped the old man into the saddle. 'I'll pull them south and then try to find Kine.'

'Use the cut behind Reeves' house,' Hopper said rapidly. 'There's a trail—keep the highest peak east straight ahead of you. That's all I know to say.'

A group of riders swung into the yard from below and Joel threw two shots at them. They faded back and a moment later one came riding in around the store and threw a torch into the yard.

Hopper spurred the black and Joel darted into the barn, feeling for the horse that should be there. He heard a frightened nicker and found the animal. It took Joel a moment to free him. The burning torch outside was sputtering out so that when he got to the door it was nearly dark in the yard again. He mounted the horse bareback, one hand tangled in its mane, and dug in with his knees. Three men were rounding the Miner's Supply and he fired at them as he urged the horse toward Reeves' house.

He got behind the small house as the shouts and the firing drew other men.

'There he goes. Watch the cut!'

He was up and into it. He slid to the ground and led the horse as the narrow trail grew steep and treacherous. Hooves rang on rock below and he turned and fired down. A man screamed and Joel went on.

He labored over the top, panting, his head pounding. From below a sudden blaze rose up, brightening the sky and highlighting the scene. They had lighted the Miner's Supply.

CHAPTER FOURTEEN

Joel pulled the horse into the brush and tied him. Then he moved behind the thick bole of a twisted yellow pine.

The burning building was throwing grotesque fingers of light into the air, reaching to the top of the cut but not beyond it.

A big roan, saddled, worked his way over the rim and into the cup. Joel crouched, puzzled at this riderless horse. And then he saw a man's denim-clad legs behind the animal and he fired, putting the bullet at the horse's front feet and sending him spooking sideways. Keno appeared, his shelter gone, and he raised his rifle.

'Back down!' Joel ordered.

Keno fired at the sound and the bullet buried itself in the tree behind which Joel stood. He fired back at the target Keno made—a silhouette against the flames from below. Keno's body teetered on the lip of the cut and then arced up and out of sight, and Joel could hear him crashing down through the underbrush.

He tied Keno's horse beside the one he had and then led his horse back to the top of the cut and slapped the animal on the rump. The horse crashed down the narrow trail, scattering men in downward flight.

He guessed that he would have an hour's start with their fear of his aim holding them back. He mounted Keno's horse and put him east on the faint trail.

He went on in as straight a line as he could, trusting the horse to feel the way, and now and then striking a match to check his position.

But soon the trail began to climb steeply, twisting, and he knew there was no going on.

He pulled off to one side and unsaddled. He slipped the bit from the horse so that he might graze in comfort, and hobbled him closely. He laid the saddle under a tree and rested against it, covering himself with the blanket.

When it was light enough for him to see the trail faintly, he saddled and rode on into the hills. By the time he topped a steep rise, he could hear the first pursuit from below. As the light increased, he could see the mountain ahead, a bare spirelike peak that was his landmark.

He stopped at a small creek to water the horse, and made his own breakfast of a cold drink and a cigarette. The soft ground at the edge of the creek showed him the clear prints of a horse and a mule, and he felt his first satisfaction.

The trail was steep in places, pitching up over rock and then twisting away into the trees.

He broke out of the forest suddenly, into a snow-filled cup that was edged by a steep cliff on the far side. A mine shaft went straight into the cliff, its opening a black mouth in the white face. Beside the shaft was a small cabin with thin smoke rising from its chimney. Joel spurred forward, keeping to the narrow trail. that was pounded into two feet of snow.

The door of the cabin opened and Kine's stocky figure stepped out. Joel held up his hands, empty, and called his name.

'Ride in,' Kine answered. When Joel reached him he grinned around the stubby pipe clenched in his teeth. 'About time,' he said.

Joel slid down and Kine caught the reins. 'Saddle up,' Joel warned. 'They aren't much over an hour behind me.' Kine waved him into the cabin. He went through the door, feeling the warmth from the stove.

Juanita came from the dim far end, stepping toward him slowly.

'Your husband is coming,' Joel said.

She stopped before him, searching his face with dark, intent eyes.

'My husband is here,' she said, and came against his chest, her face pressed to him.

When she moved back he lowered his head to kiss her, smiling down afterward. 'I thought that was why you left,' he said. 'To tell him.' She nodded, and he held her out, looking at her. 'My clothes become you,' he said.

'There's no more time for this,' she said. 'It's something we need a long while for, not just a minute snatched now and then.'

She poured out coffee and when Kine came in he sat long enough to drink a cup. Joel wolfed a piece of bannock and some cold bacon with his coffee, while Juanita busied herself with stuffing what little cooked food there was into a leather pouch.

'Where do we go?' Kine asked.

'Cardon's, if there's a way,' Joel said.

'Better trail than the one you used,' Kine said. He got up and located two rifles, giving one to Joel. 'She,' he said, nodding toward Juanita, 'is handy enough with that forty-four.'

With Kine leading on his mule and Juanita between them, they started north across the cup, picking up a trail that had been covered with a fall of snow since it was last used.

From ahead and below, a horse whinnied and the sound of men riding openly through brush came up to them. 'Cardon or Harkman?' Kine wanted to know.

'Too many for Tim,' Joel said. 'Wait here.' He slipped to the ground and went forward until he could look down. He came back and got into the saddle. 'A half dozen. And Ritchie leading.'

'To the right then,' Kine said, and reined that way.

The sounds of riders ahead halted him and he turned back. 'We're boxed,' he said. 'If Harkman scattered them like that, he's got us on three sides. We'll hit for the cabin and stand them off.'

They backtracked, pushing their horses as fast as the pitch and footing of the trail allowed. Joel was leading as they broke into the meadow and he reined back, turning his horse sideways to keep Juanita from coming into sight.

'Grotch out there,' he said shortly. 'Markle and Harkman with him.'

He estimated quickly. Harkman was as close to the cabin from his side as they were here. It was too late to run for it and, from below, came the sounds of the other crews pressing closer.

*   *   *

Jed Hopper hit Cardon's before daybreak, finding Elmira standing guard at the pass. 'Where's Tim?' he asked her. 'Abbey?'

'Tim's tuckered,' she said, 'and Abbey hasn't showed since evening.'

'You come on in,' he told her, 'and eat. They ain't following me. Joel's got 'em all excited.'

He saved his story until they were all in the house, and then told it quickly.

'As soon as it's light,' Tim said, 'I'll ride for Gil and we'll go to Kine's. If we can find the trail.'

'The shooting'll tell us,' Hopper said dryly.

'All for that woman!' Elmira said bitterly.

Hopper turned slowly, looking at Elmira. 'And worth every bit of it,' he said. 'She's a brave one, and honest. She's the kind of woman to have in your town, Elmira.'

When the first light broke, Tim went to the door. 'I'm going to see what's happened to Gil,' he said. 'We need him.'

'Joel told me to tell you Abbey found Lost Hole,' Hopper said now. He relayed Joel's story. They were all suddenly quiet. Nora Reeves rose and walked from the room.

Elmira stood up to follow Nora, and Hopper snapped at her, 'You'd do better to go watch the pass again. She needs a little aloneness about now.'

Elmira took up a rifle without a word and went out the door. She had come from the pass in a small wagon and now they could hear her get into it and ride off.

'I'll come with you, Tim,' Hopper offered.

'No,' Tim said slowly, 'I need a little aloneness myself.'

Ellen blocked the doorway when he started through it. She looked deeply into his eyes and then gave him a brief, gentle kiss and opened the door for him to go through.

He rode slowly. His pinched face was drawn with the bitterness inside him, but after a time it drained, leaving him empty.

'Ah, Gil,' he said aloud, 'she didn't want it so big and fine as all that.'

He reached Abbey's at full daybreak and climbed from his horse by the watering trough in the yard. There was smoke coming from the chimney so he knew Abbey was at home. And shortly he appeared in the rear doorway.

'Harkman's trailing Joel up to Kine's,' Tim said.

Abbey started forward and then stopped. 'How do you know?'

'Joel got Jed Hopper out of jail,' Tim said in

the same quiet tone. He shook his head. 'It wasn't any good, Gil.'

'I know,' Abbey said. 'It just built up.' He pressed his lips together and ran a hand through his yellow hair.

'Get your gun,' Tim said.

Abbey turned and went into the house, walking slowly. Tim Cardon stood by the watering trough and rolled a cigarette. When Abbey appeared again he let the cigarette hang and grow cold.

Abbey took a few short steps into the yard, his gun holstered. 'All right,' Tim said, and moved his hand. He let Abbey draw and fire and then he shot with his gun barely clear of the holster. He watched Abbey take a last step forward, his gun falling from his fingers first, and then his knees bending. Finally he crumpled forward and spread out. With an effort he turned over onto his back.

Tim looked at the watering trough where the bullet had gone in near his leg, and watched the water dribble out onto the ground. He went up to Abbey and knelt beside him.

Abbey's eyes were open and the breath came slowly from his mouth, fluttering his lips.

'Your shot was low and wide,' Tim said.

Abbey's mouth spread in a slow smile. 'Lots of little things are sometimes better than a big one,' he said.

Tim relit his cigarette and put it between

Abbey's lips. 'There's a couple drags left, Gil.'

Abbey raised a hand and steadied the cigarette, taking a deep pull. He flicked the cigarette away with his thumb and forefinger and blew out the smoke. His hand dropped over the reddening spot low on his breast, and his eyes drooped shut.

Tim stood up and walked back to his horse. He looked a long while at the watering trough before he reined around and rode away.

* * *

'We've got to run for it,' Abel Kine said. 'We make the cabin or we don't make anything.'

He spurred his mule out around them. Joel followed close behind, shielding Juanita with his horse. Markle yelled something and spurred along the trail broken in the snow. Harkman pulled past Leppy Gotch and came alongside Markle.

Juanita pulled her horse back and around Joel, heading straight for Harkman. 'Clay!' Her voice was clear and steady.

Joel saw what she meant to do and he spurred for her. Both their horses were slowed by the knee-deep snow.

Beside Harkman, Markle raised his rifle, steadying it with his good arm and drawing a bead on Juanita. Joel dug his heels cruelly into his horse's flanks and the animal pitched with its shoulder against the rump of Juanita's horse.

The crack of Markle's gun was sharp across the meadow. Juanita's horse stumbled as the weight from behind threw it and she went sideways out of the saddle and into the snow. The bullet whined over her and caught Joel's horse in the head as it reared away, fighting the snow.

Harkman watched and then he turned. He drew his gun and carefully shot Markle through the face.

Markle went backward out of the saddle and he sank out of sight in the snow. His frightened horse jumped back, floundering off to the trees.

Leppy Gotch's voice raised in a comprehending wail, 'Seth?' and he lunged his horse against Harkman's and threw himself out of the saddle, his big hands seeking Harkman's throat. For a minute they swayed on Harkman's horse and then Leppy's great weight twisted them off and they plummeted to the snow.

Joel leaped free of his horse as it fell, pulling out his gun. He pushed himself through the snow to the trail and raced up it to come alongside Leppy and Harkman.

Leppy rolled a little in the struggle and a gun barked, the impact of the bullet jarring his huge frame so that he fell clear of Harkman and half sank into the soft snow. Harkman's gun was dribbling smoke from the muzzle and it fell out of his hand as Leppy's weight was taken away.

Joel raised his gun, but there was no need. The marks of Leppy's fingers were scars around Harkman's throat and his fine head hung oddly as if he were resting it on his own shoulder.

Joel turned away. He walked to where Juanita stood waist-deep in a drift of snow, her face drawn white, her hands limp at her sides.

'Did you—?'

'No need,' he said. He saw that she did not understand. 'I would have, but Gotch broke his neck,' he added in a flat voice. 'Let me take you inside.'

Kine was calling to them. 'They ain't far off. Get in!'

Joel swung Juanita into her saddle and mounted behind her.

At the cabin, he saw Juanita into the room and then helped Kine put the animals in a lean-to shed at the rear.

Inside again, he went to the lone window, breaking its greased paper pane with the butt of his gun.

Kine said, 'I was struggling with that old mule and trying to get my gun out all at the same time—and then it was over.'

'I know,' Joel said. 'It was better the way it happened—that one of us didn't have to kill him.' He was silent a moment. 'Hear that?'

Guns were beginning to roar not far off. A

crew of horsemen poured into the meadow, running. They saw Harkman and Gotch and drew up. Kine aimed his rifle and picked the leader off his horse, and they scattered for the timber.

'Ritchie,' Joel said, watching the man who had been shot.

Three more horses broke into the clearing and swung onto the trail. Joel recognized Jed Hopper and Tim and a third who looked too small to be a man.

He threw open the door. 'Another crew somewhere,' he called. 'Watch it!'

Tim wheeled his horse and rode to them, the others following. 'That was both crews,' he said. 'We bunched them before we rode them out.' His face was inquiring, 'Juanita?'

'Here,' Joel said. Staring past Tim, he saw that the third rider was his sister. She held a rifle with smoke coming out of its muzzle.

'Where's Abbey?' Joel asked.

'Where Harkman is,' Tim said shortly. 'Let's get out of here.'

He turned back and Joel went with Kine to get the horses.

'None of them but Harkman was a fighter,' Kine said. 'They was all placer miners. They'll fade out fast enough now.'

Down on the valley floor, Joel dropped back beside Juanita. She glanced at him and then held him back with a motion of her hand so that they could come in far behind the others.

'Is that true about Abbey?'

'So Tim says,' Joel told her. 'Abbey wanted too much.'

'I wasn't thinking of him,' Juanita said. 'I was thinking of Nora Reeves.'

They rode into the yard without speaking further. He dismounted and helped her from her horse. The others had all gone in, leaving them alone.

'I'm glad you didn't have to kill him,' Juanita said suddenly.

'I would have,' Joel said.

'I know,' she said. 'He would have gone on—doing it the same way somewhere else.' She paused and added, 'If I hadn't been blind, I might have stopped him years ago.'

'How? Why was Harkman so afraid to let you live?'

She said, 'There's a United States warrant out for him in Arizona. It's nearly ten years old now but they don't forget.'

Joel looked down into her tired face. 'It's over now, Juanita. Wipe it out.' She gave him her lips, stopping further words. Then, separating, they walked to the house and into the kitchen.

Elmira Reeves was standing by the cookstove, a platter of meat in her hand. She went to the table and set down the meat. She walked up to Juanita, her eyes steady.

'I misjudged you,' she said. 'Jed told me what you did.' She put out her hand and

Juanita took it. 'I want you to stay and teach our school.' She glanced toward Joel. 'If he lets you.'

'A struggling lawyer always needs help,' Juanita said. She dropped Elmira's hand. 'Where's Nora?'

'In the bedroom,' Elmira said. 'I told her she put too much dreaming on Gil Abbey.'

Juanita's voice was gentle. 'Perhaps,' she said. 'I can help her see that a woman gets more than one chance to dream.' And smiling at Joel, she walked from the room.

We hope you have enjoyed this Large Print book. Other Chivers Press or Thorndike Press Large Print books are available at your library or directly from the publishers.

For more information about current and forthcoming titles, please call or write, without obligation, to:

Chivers Large Print
published by BBC Audiobooks Ltd
St James House, The Square
Lower Bristol Road
Bath BA2 3BH
UK
email: bbcaudiobooks@bbc.co.uk
www.bbcaudiobooks.co.uk

OR

Thorndike Press
295 Kennedy Memorial Drive
Waterville
Maine 04901
USA
www.gale.com/thorndike
www.gale.com/wheeler

All our Large Print titles are designed for easy reading, and all our books are made to last.